THE MAD MASTER

The Master of Sinanju was in a frenzy of motion, twirling like a dervish. His silver bells jingled like sleigh bells while he used his bamboo rods to describe circles in the air.

"An exorcism!" Air Force Security Officer Robin Green shrieked. "He's performing an exorcism on a nuclear facility! I'm putting a stop to this right now!"

"Uh-uh," Remo said, keeping a tight hold on her. "There was a time he was addicted to soap operas. Nobody, but nobody, interfered with his daily viewing. A couple of people did. I always had to remove the bodies."

If Chiun was going crazy, nobody was going to stop him. The only question was, how far would he go . . . and who would be left close enough to sanity to defeat a menace that defied the eye, mocked the mind, and left the Destroyer himself swinging at empty air . . . ?

The Destroyer #78

BLUE SMOKE AND MIRRORS

Created By
WARREN MURPHY & RICHARD SAPIR

A SIGNET BOOK

NEW AMERICAN LIBRARY

A DIVISION OF PENGUIN BOOKS USA INC.

SIGNET TRADEMARK REG. U.S. PAT. OFF. AND FOREIGN COUNTRIES
REGISTERED TRADEMARK—MARCA REGISTRADA
HECHO EN DRESDEN, TN, U.S.A.

SIGNET, SIGNET CLASSIC, MENTOR, ONYX, PLUME, MERIDIAN and NAL BOOKS are published by New American Library, a division of Penguin Books USA Inc., 1633 Broadway, New York, New York 10019

First Printing, October, 1989

1 2 3 4 5 6 7 8 9

PRINTED IN THE UNITED STATES OF AMERICA

For Tom Johnson, whose experiences fed this novel.

And for Marc Michaud, who kept the car in motion so the security police wouldn't have an excuse to use lethal force.

When a Titan 34-D missile exploded shortly after launch from Vandenberg Air Force Base in California, it was dismissed as an accident.

When another Titan veered off course and had to be destroyed by the range safety officer only seconds after lifting off from Cape Canaveral, taking with it a multimillion-dollar Delta weather satellite, officials dismissed it as "a short run of bad luck."

And when an Atlas-Centaur rocket went out of control during a thunderstorm, lightning was blamed, prompting a Cape Canaveral spokesman to remark that these unfortunate incidents always seemed to come in threes and no one expected any more missile accidents.

He was correct. The trouble shifted to the new B-1B Bomber program. Three B-1B's crashed during routine training missions. Everything from geese in the intakes to pilot error was cited.

The Air Force dismissed this as "expected test-performance attrition." Privately, the generals were marking time until the first B-2 Stealth Bombers rolled out of the hangars.

And when three F-117A Stealth Fighters crashed even before the first one was unveiled to the media, this was blamed on ice forming on the wings. The Pentagon sheepishly explained that the sixty-million-dollar craft were not equipped with wing de-icers—equipment common on all commercial aircraft—because they were thought unneccesary.

The Air Force generals shrugged. The next generation of Stealth fighters would have wing de-icers, they promised.

No one suspected that every one of these accidents had a common cause. No one dreamed that a single agency, unknown and unstoppable, was systematically at work. An agency that could not be touched, tasted, smelled, or heard. And one that no one had seen.

Until the day someone stole Airman First Class Emil Risko's Calvin Kleins from LCF-Fox.

They were ordinary jeans. Risko had bought them from a K-Mart in Grand Forks, paying $38.49, marked down from $49.99 "This Week Only." He brought them with him to Launch Control Facility Fox, intending to change in them after his seventy-two-hour shift. He had promised his wife that he would take her dancing at the Hillbilly Lounge. Risko folded the jeans neatly, still with their tags on, and placed them at the foot of his bunk so he wouldn't forget them.

That night, after a routine patrol of the ten Minuteman III launch facilities attached to LCF-Fox, he returned to his room and found them missing.

At first, Airman Risko thought he had placed them in a drawer. He opened every drawer. He checked under his pillow. He dug out the K-Mart bag from the wastebasket, thinking that somehow he had thrown out the jeans by accident. The bag was empty. Risko looked under the bed. He found a dustball.

After he had repeated these checks five times each, going so far as to take the grille off the window air conditioner, in the hope that someone playing a practical joke had hidden them inside, he sat down on the edge of his neatly made bunk and smoked two Newports in a row while the sweat crawled down his face.

Finally, reluctantly, Airman Emil Risko went to the facility manager's desk.

"Sarge, I have a problem."

The facility manager looked at the constipated expression on Risko's face and dryly remarked, "Ex-Lax works for me."

"This is serious, Sarge."

The FM shrugged. "Shoot."

"I bought a pair of blue jeans on the way in this morning. I know I put them on the bunk. At least I remember doing that. I locked the door after me. When I got back"—Risko took a breath and whispered—"they were *gone*."

"Gone?"

"That's right. They must have been stolen."

Staff Sergeant Shuster took a long slow puff on his cigar. He blinked several times dully. Wheels were turning in his mind, but he was slow to say anything. He looked like the Pillsbury Doughboy in Air Force blues.

"Do you now what this means?" Risko hissed impatiently.

"Do *you* know what it means?" Staff Sergeant Shuster shot back.

"Of course! It means there's a thief on the facility."

"Maybe yes. Maybe no," the sergeant said, peeling several bills off his bankroll. "How much?"

"It's not the money. They were stolen. On the facility."

"Look, they're only a pair of jeans. Do us both a favor. Take the money. Buy another pair. Forget it."

"Sarge, regulations expressly say that this has to be reported under the program."

"If you want to report this to the flight-security controller, I can't stop you. But think ahead two steps. You report this thing, and OSI becomes involved. Then everyone from the cook to the status officers in every underground LF gets hauled in for questioning.

Including yours truly. If no one owns up to it, we're all on the hook. The Air Force can't afford to have a thief on a nuclear facility. We'll all be transferred. Me, I like it out here. It's flat and out of the way, but they leave me alone."

"But, Sarge—"

Staff Sergeant Shuster stuffed a pair of twenties into Airman Risko's blouse pocket. He buttoned the pocket.

"Do it my way," he said soothingly. "We'll all have less grief, huh? You're not exactly the most popular guy on the LCF. Catch my drift?"

Airman Risko expelled a disappointed breath. He dug out the twenties and slapped them on the desk.

"Thanks, but no thanks," he said, stalking off.

"Don't do anything we'll all regret, kid," the facility manager called after him.

His face anguished, Airman Risko walked through Launch Control Facility Fox's homey recreation-room area, where other airmen were playing Missile Command, reading books, or watching television. Two airmen playing chess looked up when he entered. One cleared his throat audibly. The buzz of conversation abruptly died and Risko hurried down the corridor to his room.

The FM had a point. If he reported the theft, that meant a breakdown in the Personnel Reliability Program. It had been the first thing drummed into Risko's head when he was assigned to security detail on the missile grid. Because of the potential risks of an accidental missile launch caused by an unstable person, everyone watched everyone else for any sign of attitude or emotional changes. The officers watched the enlisted men, and each other. The enlisted men were allowed to report personality changes in any officer, regardless of rank.

Risko's bunkmate had been relieved of duty only last summer when he expressed suicidal thoughts. Risko had reported him. The man was interrogated and it came out that he had been having trouble with his wife. He suspected her of cheating on him during the long three-day shifts everyone in the grid put in. He was summarily transferred to Montana's inhospitable Malstrom Air Force Base.

Every one of the officers assured Risko that he had done the correct thing. But many of the enlisted men began avoiding him. He heard the word "fink" whispered a time or two behind his back.

Now he faced a similar situation, and although his duty was clear, Risko hesitated.

As he turned the corner to his room, his eyes cast downward, Risko bumped into someone.

"Whoa there, airman!"

"Oh, sorry," Risko mumbled, looking up. It was the new cook, Sergeant Green. She was the only woman on the LCF. That alone would have made her stick out. She was a pert little redhead with laserlike blue eyes. She wore a white cook's uniform with silver-and-blue chevrons on her collar. But Risko wasn't looking at her chevrons. He was looking at her chest. Half the LCF had bet the other half that Sergeant Robin Green had a bigger chest than Dolly Parton. No one had yet figured out a way to prove this belief to the satisfaction of the lieutenant who held the betting money in trust.

Sergeant Green looked at him sharply.

"Is there something wrong?" she demanded.

"What? No," he said quickly. "Excuse me." Risko brushed past her hurriedly. He shut the door after him, thankful for once that he had no roommate. He sat down to think.

The knock at the door came before he had a chance to light up.

"It's Green," the voice called through the door.

Airman Risko muttered something under his breath and let her in.

"OSI," Green said sharply, flashing a security ID. It

featured her photograph and the words "Office of
Special Investigations," but as was customary, no indication of rank.

"You?" he said stupidly, stepping back to let her in.

"I've been assigned to look into some problems on
the facility," Green said briskly. "And you look like
you have one of your own."

Risko shut the door woodenly.

"I don't know what to do, Sarge—I mean sir. Do I
call you sir, sir?"

"You know OSI ranks are classified. Call me ma'am."

"Yes, ma'am. You see, the regs are clear on this,"
Risko said, spreading his hands helplessly. "But it's
going to cause hell."

"Spit it out, airman."

"Yes, ma'am. It's simple. I bought a pair of blue
jeans. I put them right here. At the foot of my bunk.
Then I went on duty. When I got back, they were
gone."

"I see. There's no chance you misplaced them?"

"I turned this room upside down a dozen times."

"Who's your roommate?"

"I don't have one," Risko said miserably. "He got
transferred. It was my fault. That's why I don't know
what to do."

"Damn," Robin Green said, pacing the floor. Risko
noticed that her white uniform seemed two sizes too
small. Especially above the waist. Her buttons looked
ready to pop. A brief interest flickered in his eyes, but
the sick fear in the pit of his stomach seemed to creep
up to his eyes, dulling them.

"Airman, you strike me as a solid kind of guy. I'm
going to level with you."

"Ma'am?"

"LCF-Fox is troubled. Deeply troubled. Critical missile parts are missing from the stores. Guidance-system
components and computer parts. Technical stuff I don't
even understand. We've run countless checks, quietly

put a few people through lie-detector tests. But no leads. No confessions. Nothing. All we know is that the trouble is localized. No other LCF or LF in the grid has had problems. Only Fox."

"You think this is related to my problem?"

"My superiors are on my cute little ass—if you'll pardon the expression—to uncover a bad apple in this barrel. But I don't think we have a bad apple."

"Then how . . . ?"

"It's not a breakdown in the Personnel Reliability Program. It can't be."

"But it has to be. Nobody just walks on a launch-control facility unless he has clearance."

"I can't explain it, but I feel it in my North Carolina bones. OSI wants to pull me off this assignment, but I can bag this guy. I know it. But I need your help."

"Name it."

"I'm gonna wrangle you a pass. You go buy another pair of jeans. Let's see if he snaps at the same bait twice."

"I don't see how he'd be crazy enough to come back after getting away with it once."

"He's come back seven times to pilfer missile parts. He's a creature of habit. This is the fourth time he's gone after noncritical stock."

"Fourth time?"

"I work in the kitchen. We've been losing steaks. Sometimes two or three a night."

"Steaks?"

"From a locked walk-in freezer, airman. Twice on nights when I sat outside that locker, all night, pistol in hand. I never slept. Hell, I never even blinked. But in the morning there were two steaks missing. Porter-house."

"How is that possible?"

"I don't know if it is. But it happened. I haven't reported it. Without bagging the guy, you know what would happen to me."

"Section Eight, for sure."

"Okay, you get those jeans. Bring them back here. When you go on duty, I'm going to be under your bed waiting for this guy."

OSI Special Agent Robin Green waited five hours for the doorknob to turn. It was cramped under the bed. There was not enough room for her to lie on her side. Lying on her back was comfortable except that every time she exhaled, her blouse kept hanging up on the bedsprings. A couple of times she had to pinch her nose shut to keep from sneezing. Dust.

She never heard the doorknob turn. She had one eye on the slit of light that marked the bottom of the door. It never widened, never moved, never changed, except when someone walked out in the corridor and interrupted the light.

The hours dragged past. Robin Green grew bored; her nerves, keyed up for hours, started to wind down. She was yawning when she glanced at her watch and saw that it was 0200 hours. She shifted under the bed and happened to turn her head.

She saw the boots. They were white, with some kind of jigsaw golden tracery all over them. They were just there. For a moment they looked faint and fuzzy; then they came into focus. Robin Green thought it was her eyes coming into focus.

The hair on Robin's arms lifted. She could feel the gooseflesh crawl. She could never recall being so afraid. No one had opened the door. She was certain about that. And there was only one door into the room.

Then a voice spoke in an eerie, contented tone.

"Krahseevah!" it said. "Calvin Klein." The voice seemed particularly pleased.

She pulled her sidearm, tried to cock it, but her elbow cracked on the bedsprings.

"Damn!" she cried, struggling to squirm out from under the bed. A blouse button hung up on the springs.

She tore it free. But another one caught. She cursed her mother, who had bequeathed Robin her D-cup genes.

When Robin Green finally tore free, she rolled into a marksman's crouch. She swept the room with her automatic. Nothing. No one. Then she blinked. Something was on the wall. Then it was gone.

Robin ran to the wall and ran her fingers over the wallpaper. The wall was cool to the touch. There was nothing there. The paper was unbroken, the wall whole. She banged on it. Solid. It was not hollow. There was no secret door.

Yet a moment before, she had seen a car battery disappear into the wall. At least, it looked like a car battery. It was moving so fast, it was blurry and indistinct.

Robin Green felt the gooseflesh on her arms loosen. Then she snapped out of it. She plunged through the door and called security on a wall phone. A Klaxon began howling.

White-helmeted security police came running. They stopped in their tracks when they saw Robin Green, automatic in hand, her cleavage spilling out of her torn blouse.

"Intruder on the facility," she called. "Search every room!"

"One minute, Sergeant."

"OSI special agent," Robin Green corrected, flashing her ID card. "Now, get moving!"

"No, you hold on," one of the SP's said firmly. "Let's hear your story first before we turn the LCF upside down. How did you rip your blouse?"

"I was hiding under the bed, waiting for him."

"Who?"

"The thief."

"Thief? Who is he?"

"I don't know. I only saw his feet. He wore white boots."

"This isn't your room." The SP tapped the half-open door with his truncheon.

"It's Risko's. He let me use it."

"You and this Risko—how long have you known him? You just friends?"

"Damn this chickenshit Personnel Reliability Program! There's a thief on this LCF and he's getting away. Get Risko. He'll corroborate my story."

They brought Risko, who nervously told his story.

The entire facility was put on maximum Threatcon. Security-alert teams were deployed and every room was searched. The elevator leading to the underground missile-capsule crew was sealed off.

By sundown the entire perimeter had been thoroughly searched. No one was found who wore white boots. Nor were Airman Risko's missing jeans found. But an inventory of the locked freezer indicated that two more steaks were missing. Porterhouse.

OSI Agent Robin Green sat in the flight security controller's office, her arms folded over her torn blouse. No one would let her change, even though as far as anyone knew, she outranked most of the officers. She shivered. In the next chair, Airman Risko cast quick, hunted glances in her direction.

"We're in pretty deep, aren't we?" he muttered.

"Worse than you think. I haven't told them about the car battery yet."

2

His name was Remo, and all he wanted was to enjoy a Saturday-afternoon ballgame.

Remo sat on a tatami mat in the middle of the bare living-room floor in the first house he had ever truly owned. The big projection TV was on. Remo enjoyed the projection TV because his eyes were so acute that he had to concentrate hard not to see the scanning lines change thirty times each second. This was a new high-definition TV. Its scanning lines changed sixty times a second.

It was a legacy of years of training in the art of Sinanju, the sun source of the martial arts. One of the many downsides he had come to tolerate.

Remo thought it was ironic that the more attuned his mind and body became to the physical universe, the more trouble he had with manmade technology. He first recognized that this could be a problem when, in the early years of his training, he did a harmless thing. He happened to eat a fast-food hamburger.

Remo nearly died of monosodium-glutamate poisoning.

After that, he found it hard to watch movies. He had never thought much about how film worked before—how the illusion of action was created by light shining through the rapidly moving picture frames. Movies, of course, did not actually move. They just seemed to, much the way old flip-action book drawings appeared to move when the pages were fanned. The human eye read the changing images as action.

Remo's more-than-human eyes read them as a series of stills. Only the sound was uninterrupted. Over the years, Remo had learned to adjust his vision so that movies still moved for him, but the concentration required sometimes gave him eyestrain.

Television was the same. The pixels—the tiny phosphorescent dots of light which changed every one-thirtieth of a second—created the illusion of moving images. In fact, it was a lot like movies, which changed at a mere twenty-four frames a second, and Remo had to learn to adjust to that phenomenon too. Sometimes he could see the pixels change, line by line, on old TV's. It was distracting.

He didn't have quite as hard a time with high-definition TV's.

And so he sat down with a bowl of cold unseasoned rice and a glass of mineral water, to enjoy the national pastime. He looked like any American on this Saturday afternoon. He was a lean young man of indeterminate age, with chiseled but not too handsome features set off by high cheekbones. His brown eyes were hard as brick chips. His chinos were gray and his T-shirt was white.

Millions of other Americans had their eyes glued to millions of TV sets across America on this ordinary day. Remo liked to think he was one of them. He was not. Officially, he no longer existed. Unofficially, he was the sole enforcement arm for CURE, the supersecret government agency created to fight crime and injustice outside of constitutional restrictions. Professionally, he was an assassin.

It was a peaceful day in early autumn. The leaves had only started to turn brown and gold outside the windows of his suburban Rye, New York, neighborhood. The air was crisp, and Remo had left the windows open so he could hear the last birds of summer twitter and cheep.

A pleasant afternoon.

He knew it was not going to last when the familiar padding of sandals came from one of the bedrooms.

"What is it you are watching, Remo?" a squeaking voice asked. There was a querulous undertone to the question. Remo wondered if he had disturbed the Master of Sinanju's meditation. No, he recalled, Chiun usually meditated in the morning. Chiun had trained him in Sinanju, making him, first, more than human, and ultimately the sole heir to a five-thousand-year-old house of assassins, the first white man ever to be so honored.

"Baseball," Remo said, not looking up. No way was Chiun going to ruin this day. No way. "It's Boston versus New York."

"I knew it would come to this," Chiun said sagely. "Though you often spoke with pride of America's two-hundred-year history, I knew it could not last. It is a sad thing when an empire turns on itself. I will pack for us both. Perhaps the Russians will have use for our mighty talents."

"What on earth are you talking about?" Remo asked.

"This. Intercity warfare. A terrible thing in any age. Who is winning?"

"New York. And it's not warfare, Little Father. It's a game."

"A game? Why would you watch such a thing?" asked Chiun, reigning Master of Sinanju. He was an elderly Korean with the bright hazel eyes of a child.

"Because I'm a masochist," Remo said, knowing the humor would be lost on the man who had trained him to such a state of human perfection that he was reduced to subsisting on rice and focusing all his attention in order not to see the pixels change.

"Is this the game all Americans watch?" demanded Chiun, whose parchment features were hairless but for thin wisps of hair clinging to his chin. Two cottonlike puffs adorned his tiny ears.

"Yep," Remo replied. "The national pastime."

"I think I will watch it with you," said the Master of Sinanju. He settled at Remo's elbow like a falling leaf. Except that a leaf would make a sound hitting the floor. Chiun did not.

Remo noticed that Chiun wore his chrysanthemum-pink kimono. He tried to remember why that was significant.

"You were so quiet in there I thought you were busy," Remo remarked.

"I was writing a poem. Ung, of course."

"Uh-huh," Remo said. And he understood. Chiun was writing poetry and Remo had interrupted with his baseball. Well, Remo had as much right to watch baseball as Chiun had to write poetry. If Chiun expected total silence, then he could go outside and do it under the trees. Remo was watching this game.

"I have just completed the 5,631st stanza," Chiun said casually as his face screwed up. He, too, had to focus so as not to see the pixels change.

Remo took a sip of water. "Almost done, huh?"

"I may be almost done when I come to the 9,018th stanza. For this is a complicated Ung poem. It describes the melting of the snowcap on Mount Paektusan."

"Korean mountains aren't easy to describe, I'm sure," Remo said politely. No way, he vowed silently. He was watching this game.

"You are very astute. Tell me, I am curious about this ritual which fascinates whites so. Explain it to me, my son."

"Couldn't we wait until it's over? I'd like to enjoy it."

"I would like to enjoy my declining years," Chiun said sharply. "But I was forced to come to this strange land and train a white man in the art of Sinanju. I could have declined. I could have said, no, I will not.

And had I been so selfish, you, Remo Williams, would not be what you are now. Sinanju."

The memories came flooding back. Fragments of Remo's past life danced in his head. His youth as an orphan. Vietnam. Pounding a beat in Newark. Then, the arrest, trial, and his execution in an electric chair for a murder that was not his doing. It was all part of a frame engineered by Dr. Harold W. Smith, the head of CURE. It provided CURE with the perfect raw material, a man who didn't exist. Chiun's training had provided the rest. He shut out the memories. It had been long ago. These were happier days.

Remo sighed.

"Okay," he said, putting down his rice. "See the guys in the red socks? Those are the Red Sox. That's their name on the screen."

" 'Socks' is not spelled with an X," Chiun pointed out.

"It's just their name. They spell it that way because . . ."

Chiun's eyes were bright with anticipation. "Yes?"

"Because," Remo said at last. "That's all. Just because. The other guys are the Yankees."

"Should they not be called the Black Sox? With an X."

"The Black Sox is a whole different story," Remo said dryly, "and if we get into that, we'll be here until the year 2000. But in your own way I think you're catching on."

Chiun smiled. "The Yankees are the ones who are hurling balls at their opponents?"

"Absolutely correct. But only one of them is pitching right now. They take turns."

"And what is the purpose of this pitching?"

"They're trying to strike out the player who's up at bat."

"He is the one with the club?"

"They call it a bat."

"Why? It does not have wings."

Remo sighed again. "Look, just give me the benefit of the doubt on terminology. Otherwise we *will* be here until the year 2000."

"We will save the elaborate details until I have mastered the fundamentals," Chiun said firmly.

"Good. Now the pitcher tries to strike out the batter."

Chiun watched as the pitcher threw a fastball. The batter cracked it out to left field. Infielders scrambled for it. The batter ran to first.

"I think I understand," Chiun said levelly. "The pitcher is attempting to brain the batter. But the stalwart batter uses his club to fend off the villain's cowardly attacks. Because he was successful, he is allowed to escape with his life."

"No, he's not trying to hit the batter. He just wants to get the ball past him. If he does it three times, it's called an out and they retire the batter."

Chiun's facial hair trembled. "So young?"

"Not permanently. They just switch batters."

"Most peculiar. Why is this new person taking up a club?"

"The first batter has earned the right to go to first base. That's the white pad he's standing on there. Now the second batter is going to do the same thing. If he hits the ball correctly, he gets to go to first and the second guy will go to second base, or maybe third if the first one hits the ball far enough."

The batter swung and missed. Then he popped a f' ball into center field. Two Yankees collided in an attempt to catch it. The ball slipped between their meshed gloves.

"See!" Remo shouted excitedly. "He's going for second. He's at third! Now he's going home!"

The first batter slid to home base in an eruption of dust. The second was tagged running for third base.

The Master of Sinanju absorbed all this in passive

silence. Then he nodded. "He is going home now," he said, "his work done."

"No. He's gone to the dugout. He's already been home."

"He has not!" Chiun flared. "I was watching him every minute. He ran from third base to fourth base, and now he is walking away, dirty but unbowed."

"That's not fourth base. That's home."

"He lives there? The poor wretch."

"No," Remo said patiently. "Home plate is the object of this game. You hit the ball so you can run the bases and reach home."

"But that man started off on the home plate. Why did he not remain there, if he coveted it so?"

"Because you don't win unless you run the bases first," Remo said in an exasperated voice.

"I see. And what does he win?"

"He doesn't win. The entire team wins. They win points, which are known as runs."

"Ah, diamonds. I have heard of the famous baseball diamond. It must be exceedingly precious."

"Not diamond points. Points. You know, numbers."

"Money?"

"No," Remo said patiently. "Numbers. See the score at the bottom of the screen? The Red Sox just went from four to five. The score is now twenty to five."

"Numbers? Not gold? Not jewels? Not riches?"

"Actually, these guys make a fair piece of change. I think that batter pulls down almost two million a year."

"Points?"

"No, dollars."

"American dollars!" Chiun cried, leaping to his feet. "They pay him millions of American dollars to run around in circles like that!"

"It's not the circles, it's the points. It's the achievement."

"What do these men make, what do they build,

what do they create that they are worth such money?" Chiun screeched.

"Baseball is a skill," Remo insisted.

"Running in circles is not a skill. Beheaded roosters do it even after they are dead."

"Will you please calm down? Wait until I finish explaining the game before you get upset."

Chiun settled back onto the floor.

"Very well," he fumed. "I am very interested in learning more about these inscrutable white customs of yours."

"Now, see this batter? While you were jumping up and down he swung twice and missed. Each miss is called a strike."

"I see. If he fails to defend his home from the aggressor, his fellow warriors punish him with their clubs."

"No, a strike means a . . . There! See? He just struck out."

"And look!" Chiun proclaimed. "The opposing forces are rushing to attack him. I see now. They are going to pummel him into submission, thereby conquering his territory."

"No, that's not it. Will you let me tell it, please? They're changing sides. Now it's the Red Sox's turn to pitch and the Yankees' at bat."

Chiun's parchment face wrinkled up. "They are surrendering their opportunity to make points?"

"Yep."

Chiun clenched his bony fists. "Unbelievable! They have all the clubs and yet they let their mortal enemy take over. Why do they not beat them back? Why do they not simply crush their skulls and run around in circles as much as they wish? Thus, they could achieve thousands of useless points after they have eliminated the other team."

"They can't. It's against the rules."

"They have rules?" Chiun's voice was aghast.

"Yes, they have rules. It's a game."

"All games are a form of warfare. Chess is one example. And Go another. And intelligent men know that in war there are no rules. With such wealth at stake, they should be defending their position to the death."

"Now, how can they have a contest if they don't let the opposing team have their turn at bat?"

"Did the Greeks allow the Persians to take over their cities?" Chiun countered. "Did Rome cease laying waste to Gaul, and then stand idle while the enemy besieged their own cities so the ultimate victory would not be excessively decisive?"

"It's a freaking game, Chiun."

"It is base. Now I know why they call it baseball. It is a pastime for idiots. They run around in circles for no purpose and are paid richer than royalty. More than an assassin. Why am I not paid this richly? Do I not perform a more important service in this land of cretins? Without me, your American civilization would crumble. Without me, your feeble Constitution would be only a scrap of yellowing paper."

"Louder," Remo muttered. "The neighbors might not hear you clearly."

"I am going to speak to Emperor Smith about this at our next contract negotiation. I demand parity with these base baseball cretins."

"You may not have long to wait. I think I hear knocking at the back door."

"Some journeyman, no doubt," Chiun sniffed.

"No," Remo said suddenly, getting up. "I think it's Smith."

"Nonsense. Emperors always employ the front entrance."

"When Smith accepts that he's an emperor, and not the head of the organization we work for, I'll believe you," Remo said, angrily shutting off the TV on his way to the kitchen.

Remo opened the back door on a lemon-faced man in a gray three-piece suit and striped Dartmouth tie. His rimless glasses rode his patrician face like transparent shields.

"Hi, Smitty," Remo said brightly. "Here to complain about the noise?"

"Quick, Remo," Dr. Harold W. Smith, the director of CURE, said. "I mustn't be seen by the neighbors."

Remo shut the door behind Smith.

"Oh, for crying out loud, Smitty. We're next-door neighbors now. You can afford to be seen paying a social call."

The Master of Sinanju entered the kitchen and bowed once, formally. His expressionless face was a mask.

"Hail, Smith, Emperor of America, where hurlers of balls are paid more richly than anyone. Including those closest to the throne."

Smith looked at Remo. "What is he—?"

"I've been explaining baseball to him. He was fascinated by the players' salaries."

"Does that mean what I think it means?" Smith asked in a raspy voice.

Remo nodded grimly.

Smith turned to Chiun anxiously.

"Master of Sinanju, I realize it may seem out of line that baseball players are paid what they are, but you have to understand the circumstances. They are paid out of commercial revenues."

"Then we will do the same," Chiun shot back triumphantly. He raised a finger from which grew a long sharp nail. "I can see it now. We will fly to the ends of this disintegrating empire and after dispatching the enemies of America, Remo will shout for all to hear that this assassination was brought to you by Chocolate Frosted Sugar Bombs, breakfast of assassins."

"Oh, my God," Dr. Harold W. Smith said hoarsely.

"I'll talk him out of it," Remo whispered. "Relax, Smith. What's that in your hand?"

Smith looked down at the measuring cup clutched in his hands as if seeing it for the first time. His knuckles were white. He relaxed. His pinched sixtyish features registered doubt.

"Er, oh, this. I told my wife I was going to borrow a cup of sugar."

"Smitty, you know we don't use sugar."

"It slipped my mind. Well, that isn't the real reason I've come. We have a situation on our hands. A very bizarre one."

"Pull up a chair, Smitty. You look pale. Paler than usual, I mean."

"Thank you," said Smith, taking a seat at the kitchen table. Remo and Chiun joined him. Chiun folded his hands on the table. His expression was impassive.

"I don't know how to tell you this," Smith began. "I don't believe it myself, but the President specifically requested that I bring you into this."

"He is very wise," Chiun said blandly. "And healthy, one trusts?"

"Yes, of course. Why?"

"Chiun caught the Vice-President on TV," Remo remarked dryly.

"Youth is overvalued in this country," Chiun said. "It is another of its deficiencies."

"That is not our department," Smith said quickly. He stared into the glass measuring cup as if peering into his own grave. "We have a low-level crisis at a launch-control facility attached to the Grand Forks Air Force Base in North Dakota. They have been plagued by a rash of unexplained thefts."

"Don't tell me someone lifted a warhead?" Remo said.

"No. But critical missile parts are missing. As are certain other . . . things."

"Which things, Emperor?" Chiun asked interestedly.

"Steaks. Blue jeans. Nonmilitary items such as those. The jeans disappeared from a secure building. The steaks from a locked and watched freezer in that same building. It is impossible."

"We did not do it," Chiun said quickly.

"Master of Sinanju?" Smith said.

"When people whisper of the impossible, the name Sinanju always comes to mind first."

"I think I detect a commercial coming on," Remo groaned.

"Hush," Chiun admonished. He addressed Smith in deferential tones. "What you describe is not impossible. I could accomplish such things. Remo, too, on one of his more alert days."

"Thanks a lot," Remo said, folding his bare arms.

"But we did not. I assure you."

Smith nodded. "There's more. We have a witness to one of the thefts. An Air Force OSI agent named Robin Green. She saw the thief's feet—or what we presume are his boots. He wore what she describes as shining white boots."

"What else?"

"I am afraid that's all we have."

"Not very observant, is she?" Remo remarked.

"She was hiding under a bed at the time. When she got out, there was no one there. But in her official report she insists that she saw something disappear through a solid wall."

Remo's bored expression grew interested. "Is that so?"

"She . . . um . . . insisted it was a car battery."

"Stuff disappearing from locked rooms. Things flying through walls. It doesn't sound logical," Remo said.

"Yet these thefts have continued with impunity," Smith went on. "It's as if the thief has no fear of capture. He's never been clearly observed. He might as well be a ghost."

Remo grinned. "Well, we know that's out. We don't believe in ghosts, do we, Little Father?"

When the Master of Sinanju didn't reply, Remo turned and saw Chiun's grave face.

"Do we?" Remo repeated.

"We do," Chiun said flatly. His face was tight.

"Well, I don't," Remo snapped. "There are no such things as ghosts."

"How can you say that?" Chiun asked tartly. "You who have beheld the Great Wang with your own eyes."

"Great Wang?" Smith said blankly.

"It's not like it sounds," Remo said quickly. "Wang was the greatest Master in Sinanju history. He died a long time ago. But I met him once."

"Yes," Chiun said imperiously. "All Masters since Wang are not considered to have achieved full Masterhood until the spirit of Wang appears before them."

"Really, Remo?" Smith said, his voice level with interest. "You saw a ghost?"

"I never thought of him as a ghost," Remo replied uneasily. "It happened back during that business with the Russian superhypnotist, Rabinowitz. Remember? He had you going too."

Smith swallowed. "Yes," he said, wincing. The Russian could make himself appear to be a trusted person. To Smith, he had appeared in the form of his firstgrade teacher, and Smith had accepted this even though Miss Ashford had been dead for years. It had been very embarassing.

"Wang appeared before me," Remo was saying. "I talked to him. We had a conversation. But he wasn't a ghost. He wasn't white, didn't wear a sheet or rattle chains. He was just a fat little guy with a happy face. It was kinda like having my long-lost Korean uncle drop by for a visit. He had a great sense of humor, as I recall."

"Really?"

"Yes, really," Remo barked. "Don't look at me like that, Smitty. I can't explain it, but it happened."

"I can," Chiun said sternly. "The spirits of past

Masters of Sinanju live on after their bodies. Sometimes they return to earth to communicate. Wang has been very conscientious about that. I saw him when I reached my peak. Remo has seen him. And Remo's pupil, if he ever fulfills his duty and sires a proper son, will see Wang. It is the way of Sinanju."

Smith blinked owlishly behind his rimless eyeglasses.

"I don't know what to say," he said at last. "I do not credit the existence of ghosts. Yet these incidents at Grand Forks defy explanation. Why would a ghost haunt a nuclear-missile grid? Why would he steal such a bizarre assortment of items?"

"Maybe it's a poltergeist," Remo said with a chuckle. "Do we believe in those, Little Father?"

"Possibly," Chiun said vaguely. "I am only acquainted with the habits of Korean spirits."

Smith cleared his throat. "The President wants you both to go to North Dakota immediately. Whether a human agency is at work or not, we feel only your abilities can solve this problem." Smith extracted a sheaf of thin papers from his gray coat and placed them on the table. "This is a copy of the official OSI report on the incidents, as well as precise instructions for entering the facility. Please commit them to memory and eat them."

Remo and Chiun looked up from the paper with blank expressions. Remo fingered the thin top sheet.

"Rice paper," Smith explained. "The ink is vegetable-based."

"No chance," Remo said.

"I will see that Remo chews them thoroughly before swallowing," the Master of Sinanju assured Harold Smith as he got up to leave.

"No freaking chance," Remo repeated.

On his way out the door, Smith remembered something.

"Oh, the sugar. I would have a hard time explaining this visit to my wife if I returned empty-handed."

"We don't have any sugar, remember?" Remo growled.

"How about some rice?" Chiun suggested hopefully. "Perhaps she will not notice the difference."

"Yes, yes. That will do."

"Excellent," Chiun said, hurrying to a wall cabinet, where he went through several tins. He selected one and brought it back. He poured out a cupful of long-grain white.

"Thank you, Master of Sinanju," Smith said when Chiun stopped pouring.

"That will be seventy-five cents," Chiun said, holding out his hand. "No checks."

"Oh, for crying out loud! Let him have the rice," Remo snapped.

"I would," Chiun said sadly, "but alas, I am only a poor assassin. I am not even as well paid as a base player of balls."

"Baseball player. Get it right."

"I am sure that Emperor Smith, for all his wisdom and wealth, will not take advantage of a poor old assassin who subsists on rice and rice alone," Chiun added.

"Oh, very well," Smith said huffily, digging out a red plastic change container. He angrily counted out seventy-five cents in coins. The expression on his face was that of a man donating his critical organs.

"One last thing," Smith said on his way out. "Robin Green will be your contact. You will have her full cooperation."

"Maybe she likes rice paper with vegetable-ink dressing," Remo said with a smug grin.

Smith's face sagged. "You wouldn't."

"It's her report," Remo pointed out.

Smith left without another word.

"Can you believe that guy?" Remo said after Smith had gone. "Thinking that we'd eat his silly reports."

When the Master of Sinanju didn't answer, Remo

turned. Chiun was silently chewing, his face interested. Remo noticed that a corner of the report in
Chiun's hand was missing.

"Tasty?" Remo demanded, folding his arms.

Chiun ceased chewing. His Adam's apple bobbed
once. An expression of dissatisfaction settled over his
wrinkled features.

"It needs more ink," Chiun said, handing the report
to Remo as he floated from the room.

3

Remo and Chiun drove to McGuire Air Force Base in New Jersey, where they hitched a ride on a C-5B Galaxy cargo plane using a laminated photo ID card that identified Remo as Remo Leake, a retired Air Force captain. At North Dakota's Grand Forks Air Force Base, he produced another card that said he was Remo Overn, with the OSI. This enabled Remo to commandeer a jeep. As the Master of Sinanju watched with stiff mien and hands tucked into the linked sleeves of his blue-and-white ceremonial kimono, Remo transferred to the jeep the green-and-gold lacquered trunk that Chiun had insisted upon bringing along.

As they drove through flat North Dakota farmland, Remo broke the silence with a question:

"Is that a ceremonial robe?"

"Yes," Chiun replied tightly. His hazel eyes were agate hard. He wore a white stovepipe hat on his bald head.

"And that's not one of your usual wardrobe trunks, is it?"

"It is very special, for it contains equipment necessary for the task we face."

Remo almost braked the jeep. He swerved and kept on going.

"Hold the phone! Did you say 'equipment'? As in technology?"

"I did say 'equipment' because that is the closest English equivalent. I did not mean 'technology.' That was your word."

"If you're contemplating dismantling the U.S. nuclear deterrent while you're visiting," Remo warned, "I want you to know up front that Smith definitely would not appreciate it."

"I contemplate nothing of the kind," Chiun snapped. "And please concentrate on your driving. I wish to arrive intact."

Remo settled down to watching the road. They passed countless corn and barley fields, any of which, Remo knew, could conceal an underground launch facility and missile silo.

The access road was marked by a small sign. Remo drove the quarter-mile to the perimeter fence of Launch Control Facility Fox.

A sign on the fence proclaiming "PEACE IS OUR PROFESSION" caused Chiun to snort derisively.

The guard in the box hit a buzzer to make the barbed-wire-topped fence roll open. Remo drove in, and presented the sergeant on duty with a card that identified him as Remo Verral, special investigator for the General Accounting Office.

"Trip number 334," Remo said, repeating the information Smith had given him. "Remo Verral and Mr. Chiun."

The sergeant checked his blotter and compared Remo's ID photo against his face twice. He nodded. Then he noticed Chiun's peacocklike kimono and the lacquered trunk.

"What's in the box?" he asked.

"None of your business," Chiun said haughtily.

"That's classified," Remo said in the same breath.

The sergeant looked at them stonily from under his white helmet, then glanced at the trunk again.

"I'll have to inspect it," he said.

"Do you value your hands?" Chiun warned, withdrawing his long fingernails from his sleeves. They gleamed in the hard late-afternoon light.

"Look, pal," Remo said casually, "don't make a scene. We have clearance. You can run a metal detector along the box and trot out any sniffer dogs you have. But if he says you don't touch the box, you don't touch the box."

"I'll have to check this with my superiors."

"You do that. And while you're at it, send word to OSI Robin Green that we've arrived."

"Yes, sir," said the sergeant. He saluted just to be sure. He wasn't sure how much pull a GAO investigator had, but there was no sense taking any chances.

He came back from using the guard-box phone a moment later.

"You're free to pass, sir. Have a good day, sir."

The launch-control facility was a long concrete building. Aside from a smaller maintenance building in one corner, it was the only visible indication of a vast ICBM field that sprawled out to the borders of Canada and Minnesota.

"Before we go in," Remo told Chiun as he pulled up to the main building, "I gotta warn you. They're very touchy in installations like this. Don't antagonize them. Please. And above all, do not touch any buttons or levers or anything. You could single-handedly trigger World War III."

"Do not tell me about nuke-nuke madness," Chiun snapped as he stepped from the jeep. "I have been in these places before."

"That's right, you have, haven't you? Should I bring the trunk?"

"Later. We must examine the zones of disturbance first."

"Zones of—?"

Chiun raised an imperious hand. "Hold your questions. I will teach you the basics as we go along."

"You're the Master," Remo said.

They were met at the flight-security controller's officer by a bantamweight redhead with snapping blue eyes. Her eyes snapped even more when they alighted on Remo's T-shirted torso.

"You're Remo Verral?" she asked incredulously. She wore a regulation blue Air Force skirt uniform.

Remo pulled an ID card from his wallet, caught himself before handing over a laminated card identifying himself as Remo Hoppe, an FBI special agent, and gave her the GAO ID.

While Robin Green looked it over, Remo looked her over. He decided he liked what he saw.

Robin Green did not.

"I'm still waiting," she said hotly, "for someone to explain to me what the investigating arm of Congress is doing in the middle of an internal Air Force investigation."

Remo started to say, "Your guess is as good as mine," but decided he wanted to make a good impression. Instead he said, "This is a very, very serious matter." He hoped Robin Green wouldn't press the point. Remo didn't know squat about half the ID cards he carried. If Smith said to use one, he used it.

Robin's voice tightened. "The Department of Defense, I could understand. Or DARPA. Even CIA. But GAO?"

Remo thought fast.

"The material stolen was paid for by the taxpayers, right?"

"Well, yes," Robin Green said slowly. "So?"

"So Congress wants to know what happened."

"There's no rank on this card. You're civilian."

"Both of us," Remo said, tossing the ball into another court.

Robin Green turned to Chiun. The Master of Sinanju was looking her up and down critically. He walked behind her, as if examining her for flaws. He made a complete circle of her, saying nothing, but frowning furiously.

"Oh, this is Chiun," Remo said. "He's with Korean Intelligence."

"Korean Intelligence!"

"It's too complicated to explain," Remo said, taking back the card. "He's a specialist on loan to us. Just take my word for it."

Robin considered. "I'm a dead duck if I don't produce results pronto. It took me three days just to convince them I wasn't on drugs. So I guess I should be grateful for whatever help I can get. How do you do?" she said, shaking Remo's hand. Remo held it a few seconds longer than necessary and Robin Green's tight expression softened. Remo smiled. She returned the smile uncertainly. Worry lines still haunted her eyes.

But when she went to reach for Chiun's hand, the Master of Sinanju presented her with his austere back. He pointedly examined a plaque on the wall.

"What's his problem?" Robin asked in an injured voice.

"Technical specialists are like that," Remo said. "Preoccupied."

Chiun turned suddenly. "I would like to see the zones of disturbance," he said in a formal voice.

"He means the theft areas," Remo said in response to Robin's baffled expression.

"All right. Follow me."

As Robin escorted them down a long corridor, Remo dropped back to have a word with Chiun. It gave him a chance to check out Robin Green's walk. It was a nice walk, considering that she was in uniform. There was the suggestion of a wiggle. Not many women wiggled when they walked, he thought approvingly.

"Why did you stiff her like that, Little Father?" Remo wanted to know.

"Do not trust her, Remo," Chiun hissed back. "She is an impostor."

"Her? She's Air Force Intelligence. Smith said so."

"An impostor," Chiun repeated firmly.

"If she's a fake," Remo said, watching her hips in motion, "then I'd be interested in meeting the real thing."

"She said her name is Robin," Chiun said coldly.

"Yeah. So?"

"Robins are red."

"Yeah."

"And her other name is Green."

"Yeah?"

"Robin Green. Obviously a fictitious name. It should be Robin Red."

"Or maybe Red Robin," Remo suggested lightly.

"I saw a Robin on television once," Chiun ruminated, stroking his beard. "He was a boy. He wore very nice clothes but also a mask. He followed a fat older man, whom I suspect of leading him into evil habits. He called himself a batman, but he did not carry one of your baseball bats. He dressed like the flying bat. Obviously delusional. Like this woman."

"Uh, I'm losing the chain of this logic. Besides, this Robin's a redheaad, in case you didn't notice."

Chiun dismissed Remo's comment with a wave. "A typical white misconception, like calling brown people black. Are you all color-blind? Her hair is orange, not red."

Remo threw up his hands. "I give up."

"Mark my words, Remo. She is a fake. Do not trust her."

"I'll keep it in mind," Remo said as Robin Green came to a halt before a padlocked door. She opened it with a passkey.

"This is the room," she told them, holding the door open for them to enter. Remo noticed that her hand, resting on the knob, shook. She was still rattled by her experience.

Remo started to enter, but Chiun brushed past him.

"Polite, isn't he?" Robin remarked, arching an eyebrow.

"Don't let him fool you. He knows what he's doing. Maybe not what he's talking about all the time, but in his field, he's an expert. *The* expert."

As they watched, the Master of Sinanju padded back and forth. Remo noticed that the room was pleasant, more like a hotel room than military living quarters. There was even an air conditioner. It hadn't been like this in the Marines, Remo recalled ruefully.

"You! Female," Chiun said, suddenly turning on Robin Green.

Robin blinked. "Female?"

"Humor him," Remo whispered. "His wife was a real battleax."

"This was the room where you saw the feet of the apparition?" Chiun demanded.

"Yes. I was concealed under the bed. His feet were suddenly just . . . there. There was no sound. By the time I crawled out, he was gone."

Chiun knelt down to peer under the bed. He straightened up and examined Robin Green critically.

"I feel like a piece of meat," she whispered to Remo.

"Don't sweat it. He's a vegetarian."

"With those cowlike things," Chiun said, pointing with his long fingernails, "how did you fit?"

"What cowlike . . . ? Oh! Now, that's an impertinent question."

"I am conducting a serious investigation. Answer me."

"All right. Fine. I held my breath. Okay?"

Chiun's hazel eyes narrowed. "And the alleged car battery, where did you see it?"

"There. See the wall above the dresser? It went

through there. One minute it was plain as day, the next it was like a soap bubble. Just *pop!* And gone."

Chiun pushed the dresser set aside. It was solid maple and Robin Green was surprised at the frail Oriental's strength.

"He must eat a lot of spinach," she said wryly.

Chiun stoked the wall area with the palm of his hand.

"Here?" he demanded, turning his head.

"No, a little higher," Robin told him.

"Here?"

"I think so," Robin said slowly. Then, firmly: "Yes, there."

Chiun placed the flat of his hand to the wall. He closed his eyes and there was a long silence in the room.

"It is cool to the touch," he said, opening his eyes. "Cool, but not cold."

"I don't understand," Robin said.

"There is often a cold spot in hauntings such as this."

"Hauntings!" Robin exploded. "Wait a minute. I didn't say anything about ghosts." She turned on Remo, her eyes striking sparks. "I thought you said he was a technical consultant. What's this chickenshit about a haunting?"

"Process of elimination," Remo said quickly. "He's just eliminating a few of the less likely possibilities. He's very thorough. Honest."

"I don't believe in ghosts," Robin Green said firmly. "I never reported a ghost. I reported what I saw, nothing more, nothing less. I have a career with the Air Force, buster, and I'm not going to have my hard-earned clearances jerked because of some pint-sized Charlie Chan in a silk housedress."

"You are very excited for someone with nothing to hide," Chiun said levelly.

Robin Green turned to find that the tiny Korean was suddenly behind her.

"Look," she told him. "It took me three solid days of convincing before they let me continue this investigation. I had to pull strings like crazy, and I would never have agreed to outside help, but it was either compromise or die. I like the Air Force. I want to stay in it. I don't want to end up in a rubber room because my superiors think I've been seeing spooks."

"Remo, please tell this woman to lower her voice," Chiun said imperiously. "She is disturbing the delicate vibrations of this room." He turned on his heel.

The Master of Sinanju made a circuit of the room, sniffing the air delicately.

"This is scientific?" Robin Green asked Remo.

"He has the nose of a bloodhound," Remo answered. "What do you smell, Little Father?"

Chiun's button nose wrinkled up. "Tobacco smoke. It is ruining everything."

"This was Risko's room," Robin explained. "He was a smoker. Poor guy."

"Did he die?" Remo asked.

"Worse. They put him in charge of special projects and transferred him to Loring Air Force Base."

"That doesn't sound so terrible."

"Special-projects duty is reserved for launch-control officers weirded-out from being down in the hole too long and other emotional basket cases the Air Force is afraid to turn loose on the civilian population."

"Oh," Remo said, understanding.

"Pah!" Chiun said in disgust, joining them in the corridor. "Take me to the other places."

At the walk-in freezer, Robin Green calmly explained how, on four successive nights, she had sat in front of the big stainless-steel door waiting for the thief. "No one ever came near the place," she said. "That door was never opened, not even to inspect it during my watch. Yet steaks were missing each time."

Remo pulled on the freezer-door handle and looked in. The interior was like a refrigerator, except that a person could walk into it.

Robin Green took them to the rear, where the meats were racked. There were several thick steaks on a shelf.

"See?" she said, condensation coming from her mouth. "There's only one door. Only one way in or out. Yet somehow he—it . . . whoever—got in. And out again. It's purely impossible! How'd he pull it off, with blue smoke and mirrors?"

"Spirits do not smoke," Chiun muttered audibly as he stalked around the freezer, sniffing.

"Smell anything, Little Father?"

"No, it smells of dead animals. There is no live scent here."

"Never mind the scent," Robin Green spat. "What about getting in and out again? If there was ever a locked-room mystery in real life, this is it."

"This would pose no problem for a spirit," Chiun announced. "They are allowed to come and go as they desire. It is part of being a ghost."

"There he goes again," Robin said. She turned to Remo. "Look, you, tell me that this isn't going to turn into some kind of circus."

"Hey, don't talk to me, talk to him," Remo protested. "This is his show. I'm just an understudy."

"All right, you," Robin said, turning to Chiun. "Let's get this ghost thing out of the way right now. One: there is no such animal. No ghosts, no phantoms, no spooks, no specters or apparitions. Two: ghosts—even if they did exist—aren't substantial. They might be able to walk through a wall, but they sure can't lift a steak, any more than I could kiss a bear. And three: even if we allow for one and two, what would a ghost want with several porterhouse steaks, two pairs of size-thirty-two Calvin Klein stone-washed jeans, and an assortment of Minuteman missile parts ranging from a complete guidance package to an arming and fusing system?"

Chiun paused, his mouth half-open. He shut it. He frowned.

"She's got you there, Chiun."

Chiun lifted his troubled features.

"Show me the place from which these parts disappeared."

"Come on," Robin Green said, stomping off. Remo followed at a decorous distance.

"She is very excitable," Chiun remarked.

"You're one to talk. And what do you think of what she said? A ghost wouldn't have any use for all that stuff."

"Korean ghosts, no. American ghosts, about which I am less conversant, may be a different matter. When my investigation is completed, I may be able to offer a correct and reasonable explanation for why an American ghost would have a need for such things."

"That alone might be worth the trip," Remo said with a chuckle.

But his chuckle died as they followed Robin Green down the corridor. A Klaxon suddenly broke into song. And suddenly the halls were filled with running uniforms and worried faces.

Robin broke into a run. She flung herself into the FSC's office.

"What is it? What's happening?" she demanded.

"Trouble at Fox-4. We got a cooking bird!"

"Oh, my God!"

She pushed past Remo and Chiun as if they weren't there.

"Come on, Chiun," Remo called. They followed her out of the building. She jumped behind the wheel of Remo's jeep and got the starter working.

Remo jumped into the passenger seat, and as the jeep screeched around, heading for the gate, Remo shot a look back and saw that Chiun was running after them. He hopped aboard, and perched on top of his trunk. He clutched his stovepipe hat to keep it from blowing off.

"I suppose it's too much to hope you're not this excited because someone left a Thanksgiving turkey in the microwave too long?" Remo shouted.

Robin Green sent the jeep tearing through the gate. It rolled back just in time.

"A 'cooking bird' means that we've got a missile about to launch itself," she bit out.

"That's what I was afraid of," Remo said as rows of corn flashed past like fleeing multitudes.

4

The Minuteman III missile in the underground silo designated Fox-4 had been ANORS for two days.

Captain Caspar Auton couldn't have been happier. ANORS meant Assumed Non-operational. A computer in the underground launch facility indicated that the bird had developed a glitch. No one knew what the glitch was, but no one was worried. At any given time, five percent of American nuclear missiles were on either NORS or ANORS status—they were down or assumed to be nonoperational. It happened with a certain regularity because these devices were so complicated.

Captain Caspar Auton was launch-control officer for Fox-4. He wore the gold launch key around his neck. So did his status officer, Captain Estelle McCrone. She sat at a launch-status console identical to Auton's. It was only twelve feet away in the narrow equipment-packed room. They were paired together as part of the Air Force's new female integration program, in which women officers were paired with men wherever possible. Despite spending eight hours a day, three days a week with Captain McCrone, Auton barely knew her. Which was fine with him. She had a hatchet face and a body like a Bangladesh train wreck.

It wasn't that Auton had anything against ugly captains. It was just that he had no desire to spend his last minutes on earth in the company of one.

When the female integration program was first announced, the other male launch officers joked that when the time came, they would do their duty, then get down on the floor with their female officers and indulge in a quickie before being incinerated in their underground launch-control room.

In time of war, or when the balloon went up, as it was euphemistically known, it would be Captains Auton and McCrone's duty to remove their keys from around their necks, insert them into the paired consoles, and, after inputting the proper presidential launch codes, simultaneously turn the keys. This action would launch the Minuteman III in the nearby silo.

Today, receiving presidential authorization was far from Captain Auton's mind. He sat at his console doing crossword puzzles. He was on duty because even though the bird was ANORS, there was no way to confirm this until a technician looked it over. If a launch was called for, it was reasoned that there was no harm in attempting to launch the defective birds too. Nobody was going to be alive fifteen minutes after a first strike was called anyway. So what difference did it make?

But Captain Auton was nevertheless in a relaxed mood. He was trying to figure out a six-letter synonym for "frigid." With a mischievous smile, he penciled in the name "Estelle." The final E didn't fit, so he erased it and tried again.

He glanced over at Captain McCrone to see if she noticed his smile, when he saw her start suddenly. Her pinched face went white. Dead white. The blood seemed to go right out of it. Her mouth moved, but no words came out.

Then Auton noticed that his status board had lit up.

"L-l-launch sequence initiated!" McCrone sputtered.

"Stay calm," Auton called over. "Remember your training. We get these from time to time. We'll go through standard launch-inhibit tasks."

Frantically Auton activated a timer. According to the loose-leaf operating manual that always lay open before him, when the timer completed its short cycle, the launch sequence would be overriden.

But when the timer stopped, there was no change. The digital launch countdown was still going.

"Mine didn't take," Auton called hoarsely.

"Nothing's happening on my board either," McCrone said shrilly.

"Digiswitches! Let's go."

Flipping through his manual, Auton found the lockout codes, and with both hands reset ten small black thumb-wheel digiswitch knobs to the designated number sequences.

Nothing.

"I hope to hell you have some good news for me, McCrone," Auton said. "Because I got none for you."

"No," McCrone choked out. "What do we do?"

"Keep trying!" But Auton knew it was of no use. His board wasn't responding. The computer commands were just not taking. Somehow. Despite every fail-safe and backup. He picked up a phone handset and called the LCF.

"Situation, sir. We have a launch enable going here. We can't override."

"Keep trying," he was told. "We'll do what we can from here."

"He says keep trying," Captain Auton shouted, as he worked frantically. He couldn't understand it. His key was still around his neck. No codes had been entered. Yet the big bird was about to fly. A panel light lit up, indicating the silo roof was blowing back. She was going to fly for sure. And the last thing on Captain Auton's mind was rolling around on the floor with his status officer.

He was in a white staring panic.

The silo roof was a two-hundred-ton concrete form

set on dual steel tracks. Dynamite charges exploded, sending it shooting along those tracks as the jeep carrying Remo, Chiun, and OSI Special Agent Robin Green cleared the protective fence and bore down on the now-exposed silo in a swirling tunnel of dirt.

"The roof's blowing back!" Robin cried. She pressed down on the accelerator. The silo hatch slammed into the sandbag bulwark at the end of its short track, stopping cold.

"Shouldn't we be driving in the opposite direction?" Remo wondered aloud.

"Get ready to jump."

"What?"

"Jump! Now!" Robin cried.

"What are you going to do?"

"Just jump," Robin repeated. "Both of you!"

Remo started to turn around. "What do you think, Chiun?"

But Chiun wasn't there. Remo saw him alight in a puff of road dust. His lacquered trunk was floating down beside him. With quick movements Chiun grabbed it by one brass handle and spun like a top, redirecting its fall. It landed intact when Chiun eased it out of its orbit.

"Are you going to jump too?" Remo asked Robin.

"If I can. Now, go!"

"Suit yourself," Remo said, pushing himself out of his seat. He hung momentarily to the jeep body like a paratrooper about to hurl himself into space. In an instant, Remo's eyes read the speed of the ground moving under him, calculated the velocity with a formula that had nothing to do with mathematics, and flung himself into a ball. He spun in the air, and when he threw out his limbs, his left foot touched the ground, dug in, and Remo went cartwheeling like an acrobat. When his centrifugal force dissipated, Remo found himself standing on solid ground. He watched Robin Green send the jeep barreling toward the open silo.

Remo knew the missile lay just below the ground level, even if he couldn't see it.

The jeep raced for the silo rim. When it was on the verge of going in, and only then, Robin Green jumped.

The driverless jeep vaulted the rim, seemed to hang in the air, wheels spinning over the big circular maw, and flew like a brick. Straight down.

Remo flattened out and covered his head. He waited.

There was no explosion. The sound was more like a car crash. Then there was silence, except for the jeep's motor, which continued racing.

Remo looked back and saw that Chiun was anxiously examining his trunk. Robin Green had rolled into the shelter of an angled flame-deflector vent, and lay there with her arms clamped over her bright red hair. Presently she crawled to the silo and peered down.

"It's okay!" she called back to him.

She was on her feet and dusting off her blue uniform when Remo sauntered up to her.

He looked down into the silo. The jeep had struck the missle's white reentry vehicle and pushed it in like a punched nose. It was now wedged between the missile and the yellow silo walls, hung up on a tangle of black imbilical cables, its rear wheels spinning at high speed.

"That was pretty slick," Remo said admiringly as Robin shook dust from her hair.

"We do this all the time," she said distractedly.

"You do?"

"You'd be amazed how often we have near-launches."

"I sure would," Remo said, taking another look at the missile. It was huge. Downturned floodlights illuminated its entire length. "No chance it will launch?"

"They usually don't, but we can't take any chances. Normally we get here in time to drive a jeep or truck onto the roof hatch. The weight is enough to keep the hatch from blowing. The system is programmed not to

launch until the hatch clears. But this one went through
the sequence pretty damn fast."

"Well, that's that," Remo said casually.

"Not really. We gotta find out what caused this.
And we'd better get clear anyway."

"Why?"

"Just come on."

Remo shrugged, and followed her. As they walked
away, the silo suddenly erupted.

Remo hit the dirt, taking Robin with him. He looked
back and there was a boiling black worm of smoke
emerging from the silo. The flash had been momentary.

"What the hell was that?" Remo asked, openmouthed.

"The jeep went up," Robin said laconically.

"As long as it was only the jeep," Remo said as he
started to climb to his feet. He offered her his hand.

"And what's the idea of knocking me down like
that?" she said, slapping Remo's hand away. She
grabbed it after she struck him. "Owwwww! You're
harder than you look, for such a skinny guy."

"Special diet," Remo said, grinning.

"Just keep your cotton-picking hands to yourself,
okay? I'm a trained professional. I don't like doors
being opened for me or any of that chickenshit. I pull
my own weight."

"More than your own weight," Remo said sincerely.

"If that's some kind of sexist remark about my
bosom, I'll have you know I had heard every breast
joke ever created before I was fifteen. Twice."

"Hey." Remo said. "I didn't mean it like that."

"Sure, sure."

"No. Really. Honest."

"Save it for your report to Congress."

They approached the Master of Sinanju in awkward
silence.

Chastened, Remo attempted to lighten the mood.

"Did you see what Robin just did, Little Father?
She kept the missile from launching. Pretty brave, huh?"

"She is an imbecile," Chiun spat. "I nearly lost my trunk. It has been in my family since the days of Yui, my grandfather. Has she no respect for the property of others?"

"What did you want me to do?" Robin hurled back. "It was a nuclear emergency!"

"You might have stopped to let me off."

"There was no time!" Robin sputtered. "If that bird had gone up, the launch plume would have incinerated us all anyway."

"I am not interested in your lame excuses," Chiun retorted. "Remo, you will carry my trunk. Let us see what we can do to prevent further atrocities such as nearly happened here."

Robin Green watched the tiny Oriental walk huffily down the dusty access road, her mouth hanging open. She shut it and put a question to Remo:

"Did he understand one iota of what almost happened here?"

"Probably. Who knows? One thing I've learned is to avoid arguing with him. I never win. You won't either."

"I'll take that as a challenge," Robin said, starting off after the Master of Sinanju.

"Wonderful," Remo muttered under his breath as he hoisted the big trunk across his thin shoulders. "I think all my troubles just went ballistic."

5

The Fox-4 silo could be reached from a fenced-off access hatch in the middle of an oat field. Robin Green led Remo and Chiun down this and into the underground Field Maintenance building. They had no special clearance to enter the silo itself. So while the necessary red tape was being cut, Robin left Remo and Chiun in the missile-parts storage area.

Chiun walked around the area, sniffing.

"I smell electricity," he said at last. He was puzzled.

"Sure. All this equipment," Remo pointed out.

"It is not clinging to these machine parts," Chiun said. "It hangs in the air. It is not right."

Then Robin returned to escort them to the underground launch facility through a pair of air-lock-like hatches, down a gleaming steel tunnel to the silo itself.

They gathered at the launch platform on which the big engine nozzle sat like a great silent bell. Gray-overalled AFSC maintenance teams swarmed around them. Remo was surprised at all the corrosion and water seepage. A rat scurried behind a cable. Above them, technicians worked on maintenance platforms, opening access panels and yanking umbilical cables. Far above, where daylight filtered down, the scorched jeep was being lifted free by a chain hoist.

A technician up on a high platform pulled his head from an access panel and called down:

"Everybody can relax. This bird isn't going anywhere. It's been gutted."

"What do you mean, gutted?" Robin Green called up.

"Just what I said. Gutted. Somebody pulled out all the firmware. It's just not here."

"Let me see that," she said, climbing up to the platform.

The technician handed her a flashlight. She shone it in through the hatch. The light picked out a mass of connections and mechanical devices. Tangles of flat connector cable hung slack, like detached hoses. Tooth-like prongs gleamed hungrily.

"See? All the BITE firmware has been yanked," the technician was saying.

"Just what is that? And use small words. I'm no expert."

"BITE stands for built-in test equipment. They're mostly ROM and PROM chips mounted on cards. They perform constant diagnostic tests of the bird's systems. This explains why she's been ANORS. But it doesn't explain how this stuff disappeared from a sealed missile."

"I want a list of every man who worked around this bird since it was loaded," Robin Green said angrily.

"That's four years' worth of duty rosters."

"Then you'd damn well better get started, hadn't you? And I want it by oh-six-hundred hours."

Robin joined Remo and Chiun below.

"You were pretty tough on him," Remo remarked.

"Don't let these hooters fool you," Robin snapped, cocking a thumb at her chest. "I'm all business."

An Air Force security policeman in camouflage fatigues and an olive-drab helmet emblazoned with the Strategic Air Command crest approached.

"Begging your pardon, ma'am," he said. "The launch and status officers are being held for you in the LC, as per your request."

"Come on, you two."

Remo picked up Chiun's trunk. He tucked it under one arm, although it was obviously very heavy.

"I'm beginning to feel like the fifth wheel on this job," he complained.

"Just do not drop my trunk," Chiun sniffed, hurrying ahead of him.

In the launch-control room the launch officers nervously waited under the steely gaze of another SP in fatigues, who stood with his hands clasped behind his back. A technician was opening up one of the dual boards.

"Look," he said.

While the technician held a light steady, Robin Green examined the console's innards.

"What am I looking for?" she asked.

"The launch-inhibit module."

"Is that the boxy thing?"

"No. The launch-inhibit module is normally connected to the boxy thing. But it's not there."

Robin Green stood up. "Not there? As in missing?"

The technician nodded grimly. "Someone stole it," he said.

"Get me the duty roster of everyone who performed maintenance on this console."

"Not necessary. I was the last one to open her up."

"Do you remember the launch-inhibit module being there?"

"It was there two days ago. And I can guarantee you that no one's opened this console until a few minutes ago."

"How can you be certain?"

"Because it was the act of disconnecting the module that triggered the launch sequence."

"That means—"

"It was lifted in the last hour. Don't ask me how. Gremlins. Martians. Blue smoke and mirrors. Take your pick."

Chiun cocked an ear in the man's direction and his face grew more intent. He whispered something to Remo, who in response shook his head and hissed, "Not now."

"Where are the launch officers?" Robin shouted, turning around. "Step forward!"

Captains Auton and McCrone stepped forward sheepishly.

Robin Green shoved her flashlight into their faces. They fliched from its hard glare.

"Don't look away when I'm addressing you. Stand easy. I'm Green. OSI. Let's make this easier all the way around. You were both on duty. You sat twelve feet apart in full view of each other. Neither one of you could have lifted the module without collusion on the part of the other. Therefore, you're both guilty of theft and treason. Who wants to talk first?"

Captain Auton spoke up. "Ma'am, I had nothing to do with this. And I can vouch for Captain McCrone."

Robin frowned. "You!" she barked, switching the beam into Captain McCrone's dark eyes.

"Ma'am, I was sitting at my board, as was Captain Auton. The module may be missing from his console, but I can assure you that Captain Auton was at his post at all times."

"I see," Robin said tightly. "A pair of collaborators."

"Hold," Chiun said. "Allow me to speak with them."

"What good will that do?" Robin demanded hotly.

"I believe they speak the truth. I wish to verify this."

"And how do you propose to accomplish that?" Robin said, eyeing Chiun's scrawny arms as he shook them free of his sleeves.

"A simple interrogation," Chiun said blandly.

"That's up to OSI. This isn't your department." Robin turned to the stony-faced SP. "Guard, these two are not to interfere with my interrogation. Got that?"

The SP took a tentative step forward.

Chiun turned to Remo. "Remo."

"Gotcha, Little Father," Remo said, flashing an A-okay sign.

Remo stepped back and took the surprised guard by one wrist. He pivoted in place, sending the man slip-sliding out of the control room. Remo shut the door after him. The guard could be heard beating on the thick metal with his truncheon and blowing his whistle furiously.

"Go ahead, Little Father," Remo said calmly.

The Master of Sinanju stepped up to the trembling officers.

"Do not be afraid," he murmured. "I wish merely to speak with you. Will you answer one, possibly two, simple questions from a harmless old man?"

The pair hesitated, looking to Robin Green.

Robin shrugged. "Go ahead."

"Here," Chiun said, extending clawlike fingers. "Take my infirm old hand, if it will reassure you."

When the pair took Chiun's hand in theirs, they suddenly fell to their knees, faces twisting, their bodies writhing in agony.

"Speak now!" Chiun urged them. "Only the truth will stop the pain."

"I don't know anything! Really!" Auton howled.

McCrone shrilled that she knew nothing either.

Auton pointed out that they were locked in this control room. If either of them had lifted the module, it would still be here.

Chiun released their hands. He faced Robin Green and tucked his hands together solemnly.

"They speak the truth," he announced.

"Nonsense," she retorted.

"Check out their story, then," Remo suggested. "Have the place searched."

"I'll need the guard."

Remo released the door and the guard crashed in, his sidearm out and wavering between Remo and Chiun.

"Oh, put that away," Robin said in an annoyed tone.

When the SP hesitated, Remo relieved him of his helmet. He clamped it over the automatic and manipulated the helmet with swift finger strokes. The helmet rapidly compressed into a mashed ball that enveloped the guard's hand and weapon. The SP looked at it stupidly.

"How did you do that?" Robin Green wanted to know.

"Do what?" Remo asked casually.

"Oh, never mind," Robin said exasperatedly. She ordered the SP to go get his hand attended to.

The SP retreated from the room. Other SP's came, summoned by the first one's whistle. Robin ordered them to take apart every square inch of the room until they found the missing module.

After a three-hour search, no module turned up.

"I give up," Robin Green said morosely.

"Good," Chiun said. "Now it is my turn. Remo, the trunk."

"Over there, Little Father."

Chiun bent over his trunk and unlocked it with a brass key. He flung the lid back and came away with his hands full of what seemed to Remo like ceremonial objects.

As they watched in openmouthed amazement, the Master of Sinanju began to set crude candles at every corner of the control room. He lit them. Then he took three jars of colored fluids to the center of the room.

He poured a pinkish fluid in a dish in the middle of the floor and ignited it with one of the candles. Then he poured a blue fluid in a circle around the burning dish.

Robin Green held her nose against the stench that resulted. Remo simply keyed his breathing down so that his nostrils filtered out the most disagreeable aspects of the smell.

"What on earth is he doing?" Robin asked Remo.

"Silence," Chiun commanded.

Then the Masters of Sinanju took up two bamboo sticks that were decorated with varicolored feathers and topped with silver bells. He began to stalk around the burning bowl and his voice rose from its usual squeaky pitch to a quavering howl that reminded Remo of a lovesick alley cat.

It reminded Robin Green of something entirely different.

"What is he doing?" she asked tartly. "A rain dance?"

Remo, who knew Korean, listened for a moment and offered what he called a loose translation.

"It sounds like he's saying something to the effect of 'Begone, spirits of the outer void. Return from whence you came. Leave this ridiculous missile and the unsavory steaks and garments to the living. There is nothing here for you.' Unquote."

"An exorcism!" Robin shrieked. "He's performing an exorcism on a nuclear facility! Oh, I'm not seeing this! I'm not hearing this."

"Hey," Remo said. "I said it was a loose translation. I might have gotten a few of the words wrong."

"Well, I'm putting a stop to this right now."

Robin Green started forward. Remo caught her by the waist.

"Uh-uh," he said. "Seriously."

"Let me go, you big goof. I have authority here."

"You may have authority, but not over him. Look."

The Master of Sinanju was now in a frenzy of motion. He ran from wall to wall, literally bouncing off them. Whenever he bounced, he struck the wall with one of the bamboo rods. He leapt into the air, twirling like a dervish. The silver bells jingled like sleigh bells. Chiun seemed to be using the rods to describe invisible circles in the air.

"There was a time when he was addicted to soap operas," Remo explained. "Nobody, but nobody, ever interfered with his daily viewing. A couple of times people did. I always had to dispose of the bodies."

"Bodies! Him?"

"Parts of bodies, actually. They looked like they had walked into a baling machine or something."

"Him?" Robin repeated incredulously.

"Trust me."

"That's ridiculous! He can't weigh more then ninety pounds."

"A black widow spider weighs even less."

"Well, I don't care. This is chickenshit. And it's got to stop."

At the sound of Robin's shouted words, Chiun suddenly stopped in his tracks.

"Thank you for reminding me," he said, going to the trunk. He returned with two jars of a dark ashy substance. He handed one to Robin.

"Since you are obviously familiar with this ritual, you may help," he said. "Dip your finger into the jar and anoint first your forehead, then everything else in this room that is green. For they like green and use it to empower themselves."

"Green?" Robin croaked.

"Yes. Be certain to do your forehead first. It will protect you. Even if you are not truly green, but only named so."

"What is this stuff?" Robin asked, bringing a smudge of it to her nostrils.

"It is the chicken stuff of which you spoke, of course," said Chiun, who then marched off and began smearing ash over every green status light and indicator on the twin consoles.

Robin Green's eyes widened in horror. "Chicken . . . ? He can't mean that this . . . This isn't . . . I mean . . ."

"Search me," Remo said. "Guano isn't my area of

expertise. But maybe you'd better do as he says. You're starting to look a little green around the gills."

Robin didn't reply. Her expression was dazed.

At length Chiun finished his ministrations to the launch-control room.

"All done, Chiun?"

"No. I must do the missile too. I will do all the missiles so that the wicked ghost causes no accidental launchings."

"There are ten missiles attached to this LCF alone," Robin Green pointed out. "And fifteen LCF's in the grid. That's one hundred and fifty missile silos."

"I will start with this one. If necessary, I will do others."

"Better humor him," Remo said quickly. "The sooner we're done, the sooner we can get on with the real investigation."

"This is madness. But all right. Just let go of me."

"Huh?"

"You've still got your arms wrapped around my waist, buster. Or haven't you noticed?"

"Oh! Sorry," Remo said, his face reddening. "I just didn't want you to get hurt." He released her.

An hour later, the Master of Sinanju stepped back from the silo hatch to Fox-4. He surveyed the hatch from every angle. The entire surface was covered with arcane Korean symbols, daubed on in dried chicken guano. He had placed one of the feathered rods to the north of the silo and the other to the south. They tinkled in the breeze like wind chimes.

"Finally," he intoned, addressing a ring of security police, whom he had set to beating on their helmets because it frightened off certain kinds of spirits, "I declare this absurd contraption proof against spirits, demons, and other inhabitants of the outer void. You may all go about your business normally."

"I don't believe this," Robin Green groaned. "I'm going to be drummed out of OSI for this."

"Hey, who you gonna call?" Remo joked. When Robin Green gave him the benefit of the stoniest expression Remo had seen since visiting Mount Rushmore, Remo added, "But seriously, now that Chiun is satisfied, we can really go after this guy."

"How?"

"We know he likes steaks. Let's put a hook in one. Maybe he'll take the bait again."

"I already tried that. You know what happened."

"Did you ever wait for him inside the freezer?"

"No. I didn't dare. No one on the LCF knew I was OSI. If I got locked in, I could have frozen to death before anyone realized I was missing."

"I guarantee that I won't let that happen," Remo said, smiling broadly.

6

OSI Special Agent Robin Green shivered behind a hanging side of beef.

She clutched the white blanket around her more tightly. The blanket was white to help her blend in with the color of the butcher paper in which the assortment of pork chops, ribs, and other meats that occupied the upper shelves at the rear of the freezer were wrapped. She perched on the lowest shelf.

"I swear," she muttered, "after tonight, I'm never going to eat meat again."

"Did you say something?" Remo asked, sticking his head into the freezer. The overhead light came on automatically.

"Shut that door!" she scolded. "I was only talking to myself."

"Oops! Sorry," Remo said, shutting the door. The freezer went dark again.

How the hell did he hear me through that door? Robin thought. I spoke under my breath.

But that wasn't the most amazing thing she had seen Remo, or even Chiun, for that matter, do in the few hours she had known them.

If they were GAO, then Robin Green was PTA. But they had been cleared by the highest authorities. Robin had attempted to backtrack their clearance. The base commander at Grand Forks had informed her that it came from the Pentagon. When she attempted to trace the specific office or service branch, she was informed that their clearance didn't originate in the Pentagon. The Pentagon was only a convenient conduit.

The last Robin Green had heard, the Pentagon was not an arm of the General Accounting Office. Hell, they were mortal enemies in the yearly battle of the budgets.

It didn't figure. But there they were, T-shirts, feathered wands, and everything.

As Robin's eyes readjusted to the darkness, she shifted again. Her head struck the shelf directly above, knocking over a rack of ribs. She looked to see if the displaced ribs exposed her to view. They didn't. She pulled the blanket about her more tightly.

When she looked up, the air was filled with a soft white glow, and even under her blanket she felt the hair on her arms rise like a million saluting insect antennae.

It was there. Right in the freezer. It glowed. Its back was to her. From head to toe it was a blurry white, like a fuzzy blanket with a light under it. Except that all over its body, golden veins showed. They swam with light. It was as if this thing had veins on the outside of its skin through which light instead of blood coursed. And on its back was slung a napsacklike thing, also white. It was open at the top, with two cables coming out of it like tentacles. They looped up to connectors in its shoulders.

It was manlike, Robin saw. It had two humanoid legs and two arms—although she couldn't quite see the arms clearly. It was bent over the steak rack. The back of its head was as smooth and white as an egg. Hairless, it lacked those golden veins.

Robin Green knew the white thing had not entered by the freezer door. It could not have gotten past Remo and Chiun. And even if it had, the light would have gone on automatically. And it had not.

Unless . . . unless he had killed the electricity. No, that wasn't it, she realized. The compressors still hummed. But there was another sound. A crinkling. Rhythmic and brittle. It was like the slow crushing of stiff cellophane. It started suddenly, and Robin noticed that the fuzzy glow had faded. The white thing now resembled some glossy white creature. The golden veins had faded away. No, they were still there. But they were colorless now.

Then the apparition spoke.

Krahseevah!" it breathed.

Robin Green tried to speak. Nothing came out of her chattering mouth except cold condensation. She decided to scream.

But before she could summon up the breath for a really good yell, the apparition turned.

And then Robin Green saw the creature's profile.

It was featureless. It stuck out like a white blister. Her scream died in her throat. As she watched, the blister contracted, and Robin knew that was the source of the crinkling sound. Inhale. Crinkle. Exhale. Blister. Inhale. Crinkle. Exhale. Blister.

Every time it took in air, the blister crinkled inward. Then it ballooned out. It was breathing somehow. It was breathing even though it didn't have a nose or mouth or eyes or anything. Just a smooth featureless blister that expanded and collapsed like some gruesome external lung.

It was too much for Robin Green. She covered her head with the blanket and started screaming.

"He's here! In here! He's here!" Robin shouted.

The light went on. The door opened and Remo and Chiun were suddenly in the freezer. Robin shook the blanket off and jumped from her hiding place.

"Where?" Remo demanded, looking around.

"Right there!"

Robin pointed to the rear of the freezer.

"I don't see anything," Remo said.

"Damn! He flew the coop again!"

Chiun approached the wall, tapping it with his long fingernails. "He disappeared through this wall?" he demanded.

"I think so! What took you so damn long?"

"We were here before you finished screaming," Remo insisted.

"I did not scream," Robin said defensively. "I called for help."

"Sounded like a scream to me."

"You are such a chauvinist jerk, you know that?" Robin shouted, clutching herself. She shivered uncontrollably.

"Remo, do you smell it?" Chiun asked suddenly.

Remo sniffed the air.

"Yeah. Electricity. It's very strong."

Robin Green sniffed the air too. It smelled cold to her. Like old ice cubes.

"I don't smell anything," she said.

"There are four steaks missing," Remo said, examining the steak shelf. "The four biggest, thickest, juiciest, most succulent—"

"Remo!" Chiun admonished.

"Sorry," Remo said. "I haven't had a steak in years and years. You miss little things like that."

"Well, don't just stand there," Robin snapped. "He went through that wall. Maybe we can still catch him."

"Yes, for once this loud female is correct, Remo," Chiun said. "We will search."

They searched the entire launch-control facility. The post went to full alert. No trace of a white-skinned manlike creature with external golden veins was found.

"He must have left the facility," Robin suggested at last.

"We can split up," Remo suggested. "There's a lot of ground to cover. But we can make good time if everyone pitches in."

"Not necessary," she barked suddenly. "Come on."

Remo followed her out to the LCF perimeter. A green Air Force Bell Ranger helicopter was settling to the ground. A major stepped out, clutching his cap against the prop wash.

Robin ran up to him and said, "Major, I'm commandeering your chopper."

The major began to bluster, but Robin flashed her OSI card and he subsided.

Robin waved Remo and Chiun into the helicopter.

"Step out, airman," Robin told the pilot. "I'm rated for one of these birds."

The pilot hastily got out of the way while Robin seized the controls. She tested the cyclic control and worked the directional-control pedals while Remo and Chiun climbed aboard. The helicopter lifted off like an angry buzz saw.

"You handled that major like you outranked him," Remo said over the turbine noise. "Do you?"

"No," Robin said tartly, "but he doesn't know that."

"Oh, It's getting dark. Think we can find our phantom?"

"He was all white and he glowed. He should be easy to spot," Robin explained over the rotor churn.

"I hate to break this to you," Remo said. "But Chiun and I didn't see or hear a thing."

"He spoke. You didn't hear that?"

Remo frowned. "What did he say?"

"It sounded like 'graseeva' or something."

"I thought that was you," Remo said.

"Me? Why would I say something like that?"

"That's what I wondered. I figured maybe you were muttering under your breath again."

"You know, if you'd acted when you heard that, you'd have been in time to catch him."

"And if it was only you, you'd have bitten my head off."

Robin Green was silent for a long while as she canted the Bell Ranger in spiraling circles.

"You're right," she said finally in a quiet voice. "I'm sorry. There was something else. Something I'm almost afraid to mention."

"What's that?"

"Remember the car battery I saw go through the wall the day the jeans were stolen? Well, I just saw it again. It was strapped to the thing's back."

"Really?"

"That's not the strange part. It had a brand name on it. It was a Sears car battery."

Remo looked at Robin Green's tense profile.

"Don't look at me like that," she said tightly.

"I wonder," Chiun mused from the back of the helicopter.

"What's that, Little Father?"

"Why would an American ghost be speaking Russian?"

Remo and Robin exchanged glances.

But before either of them could ask the Master of Sinanju what he meant by that remark, Robin Green's voice lifted.

"There!" she called, pointing down. "There in that field. See? He's running."

A tiny white figure darted between rows of corn. It shone faintly, like a glow-in-the-dark light switch seen from a distance. It made for a solitary tree and popped behind it. It didn't come out again.

"Must be taking a leak," Remo remarked.

"I'm going to set her down," Robin warned them "Get on the horn and call for support."

"Glad to," Remo said, reaching for the radio. "Just tell me how to work this thing."

"Never mind," Robin said dismally as she settled the helicopter down toward the rippling grass.

7

"He's got to be up there," Robin Green said worriedly, shining a flashlight up into the thick tangle of oak branches. She held her automatic in the other hand. It was cocked and aimed upward.

The helicopter sat only a hundred yards away, its rotors whirling quietly. The lazy backwash stirred the leaves and her short red hair.

Remo stared up into the tree. "I don't see anyone," he said. "How about you, Chiun?"

Chiun walked around the thick tree bole, his parchment lips compressed in concentration. "No," he admitted.

"Well, we know he ducked behind this tree," Robin said peevishly. "I saw him. We all saw him."

"Guess so," Remo said vaguely.

"Possibly," Chiun remarked. His hazel eyes were intent on the ground.

"This is the only tree on this field," Robin said. When no one replied, she went on: "Look, let's approach this rationally. We saw him go behind the tree. He's not behind the tree. Okay. But we know he didn't run away from the tree, otherwise we would have spotted him. Ergo, he's up the tree."

"If he were up there, he would glow," Remo pointed out. "We'd see him."

"One of us should go up there to make sure," Robin suggested.

"Waste of time," Remo said, looking around the field.

"Then I'll go," Robin said, tucking her light into her belt. She uncocked her automatic and holstered it. Then she shinnied up the thick bole until she got hold of a solid branch, and levered herself into the crotch of a limb. She pulled out her flashlight, shining it this way and that.

"I take back what I said about that one," Chiun told Remo as they watched her throw light around.

"What do you mean?"

"She is correctly named. She refers to everything, whether it is an atomic missile or a helicopter, as a bird. Now she is demonstrating that she is perfectly at home perched on a tree branch. She is indeed a robin, even is she is not truly green."

"I'm sure she'll be thrilled to hear that, Little Father." Remo cupped his hands to his mouth. "See anything?" he called up.

Robin Green peered down through the thickening dusk.

"No," she said wonderingly. "I don't understand this. We all saw him go behind this very tree. But there are no footprints leading away."

"And there are none leading to it," Chiun pointed out. "Except our own."

"What?" Robin Green scrambled down the tree, agile as a monkey.

"Damn these jugs," she said, fixing her blouse. "My buttons came loose while I was up there. You'd think the Air Force would design their uniforms to take the full-figured woman into account." She looked up. "Well, you don't have to stare."

"I was not staring," Chiun said indignantly.

"I meant him," Robin retorted, indicating Remo,

who then pretended to look away. "I'll never fathom the American male fascination with boobs."

"Like attracting like," Chiun muttered. Remo shot him a withering glance.

"Now, what's this about no footprints?" Robin demanded, once more presentable.

"Behold," Chiun said, pointing to the dusty earth. The tree was surrounded by the patchwork of many feet.

"This is mine," Robin said, kicking at one set of prints."

"And these are mine," Chiun said, pressing his sandal into a delicate footprint. It fitted perfectly. "And these ridiculously large ones are Remo's, of course," Chiun added.

"No, some of them must belong to that thing," Robin countered. "We all saw him come this way. You, Remo, come with me. We'll do a process of elimination."

"Why me, Lord?" Remo asked the heavens. But he allowed Robin to lead him around the tree. Each time he stepped into one of the large footprints, it fitted. And Robin then would erase it with the heel of her boot.

When they were done, all that remained were her footprints and those of the Master of Sinanju. And a string of tracks belonging to all three leading back to the helicopter.

"No strange footprints coming. No footprints going away," Robin moaned. "How am I going to explain this? How the hell am I going to write this up? They already have a psychiatric notation in my files from the other day."

"Look, we're wasting time here," Remo pointed out. "Obviously he got away. Let's get upstairs again. Maybe we can spot him from the air."

"No. No. He came to this tree. He's still here. I don't care if he is a ghost and doesn't leave footprints. This is wide-open space. We would have seen him running off. He's somewhere around this damn tree. We just have to figure out where."

"Okay, tell me where to start looking and I will," Remo said.

"I don't know," Robin moaned unhappily.

At that moment a dusty station wagon pulled up. A farmer in overalls cranked down the window and put his seamed face out.

"Something wrong here, folks?" he drawled.

"Do you own this field?" Robin asked him.

"All but what the government took for their dang silo."

"Then I'm sorry. But I'm going to have to ask you to leave," Robin told him. "This is an official Air Force investigation. You'll be notified of the seizure."

"What seizure? What are you seizing?"

"I'm afraid I'm going to have to confiscate this tree in the name of the U.S. Air Force."

"That there tree? What's it done?"

"That's classified. Now, could you please be on your way?"

The farmer stared at them. His eyes went to Robin, then to Remo, and finally to Chiun, who stood magnificent in his blue-and-white silk kimono.

"I'm gonna have to check on this, you know," he said, putting the station wagon into reverse.

After he was gone, Remo had what he thought was a reasonable question.

"How do you confiscate a tree?"

"With chain saw and winches," Robin retorted. "Now, excuse me while I radio for equipment." She started walking back to the helicopter.

The ground shook suddenly. She whirled.

"What the hell?" she blurted, beholding a curious sight. Remo was on one side of the tree, Chiun on the other. Remo kicked at the base of the tree. It shuddered violently. Remo's foot left a distinctly noticeable dent. Then Chiun kicked at the opposite side. He kicked a little higher than Remo had. About a foot higher. His delicate sandals left a dent too. Then Remo kicked again.

As Robin Green watched with her mouth going slowly from merely parted to wide open, they switched off until the tree was poised on a thickness no larger than a strong man's thigh.

Remo stepped back and the Master of Sinanju pressed his hand against the tree. It snapped with a thunderous sound.

"Timberrr!" Remo shouted. He was grinning. It was the grin of a happy idiot, Robin thought. The showoff. Then her eyes flicked from Remo's too-wide grin to the space where the tree no longer stood.

Standing there, its feet sunk into the stump like some kind of life-sized Oscar statuette, was the thing.

"There it is!" Robin screeched. "There's the bastard!"

Remo's grin vanished. He turned.

And he saw it too. Tall as a man, a fuzzy glowing white and covered with moving streams of golden light. Its face was a bubble that collapsed and expanded even as they focused on it.

Then, carefully, silently, the thing stepped out from the stump and stalked away.

Chiun reacted first. He leaped for it, one foot extended in an attack thrust.

Remo saw the impossible. His skirts flaring, the Master of Sinanju was descending in a Heron Drop maneuver. He was going to take the thing's head right off. But when his foot seemed about to make contact, the thing continued running, oblivious of Chiun's lightning kick.

Chiun hit the ground in a ball. He snapped to his feet, his cheeks puffed out in fury.

Remo flashed past him. Chiun, racing, caught up with Remo.

"He is mine," Chiun hissed explosively.

"You missed. How could you miss?" Remo demanded. "You never miss."

"I did not miss. My foot touched him. But there was no substance to receive the blow."

"Yeah? Watch this," Remo said. He pulled out in front of Chiun. He was gaining ground on the thing, who might not leave footprints in loose dirt, but was no sprinter. It clumped along like it had flat feet.

Remo recognized the battery on its back. White cables led from it to the creature's shoulders. As Remo gained ground, the thing turned its head to see its pursuers, and Remo saw again that weird bubble of a face, soundlessly expanding and contracting like a bladder.

The white thing tried to zigzag. But its movements, for all their eerie silence, were awkward.

Remo zipped out in front of him. The creature dodged clumsily. Remo was too quick. He wrapped his arms around its waist.

"Got him!" he shouted.

But Remo's elation was momentary. He realized he hadn't connected, and the force of his leap was carrying him through and beyond the thing. Remo recovered and tried again.

The thing weaved. Remo was quicker. He tried to swat its head. The blow kept on going. Remo felt no contact. No nothing. It was like grabbing at smoke—except smoke could be disturbed or dispelled. The creature simply kept moving.

Then the thing stopped still. It folded its arms. Tucked in the crook of one arm were two steaks wrapped in butcher paper.

Chiun caught up. He took a position on one side of it, Remo on the other.

"Care to try again?" Remo asked.

"Yes. I owe this vile thing retribution for the humiliation of my fall."

"Good luck. I don't think you're going to accomplish much."

The Master of Sinanju circled the white thing warily, like a hunter before a sleeping beast. He feinted with a hand. The thing's featureless head flinched.

"Hah!" Chiun exulted. "This monstrosity fears harm. It can know pain. And if it knows pain, we need only find its weak points."

But when the Master of Sinanju attempted to knock the thing's feet out from under it, it simple stood there like a pillar of wan light. Chiun kicked again. He kicked a third time. All to no effect.

In frustration, the Master of Sinanju left off his careful circling. He stepped up to the thing and methodically tried to kick it in the shins, alternating left and right shins. He looked like a fussy little hen scratching at gravel.

The creature just stood there in silence, its blister face working noiselessly. Remo timed the contractions. They corresponded to a normal human respiration cycle. A tight smile warped his mouth. It was human enough to breathe, at least.

Remo tried a rear approach. He put his hands into the battery. They disappeared as if into milk. Remo kept his hands in there. He felt no sensations. Neither heat nor cold. There was no sound or discernible vibration. Only steady clods of dirt passing through the creature's form to land on Remo's Italian loafers.

Remo stepped around to the front.

"Might as well give up, Little Father," he told Chiun. "You're not going to make an impression on this guy."

"And what would you have me do?" Chiun said, still kicking up dirt.

"I don't know. But for once, let's try to figure this out calmly."

"I am calm," Chiun insisted as he tried to crush the

thing's toes with repeated stamping motions. All that he accomplished was to shake the ground.

Remo examined the thing from the front. He saw that its entire body was enveloped in some luminous material. It seemed to shine from within. Remo looked closer. The golden traceries, he saw, were less like a web than veins. They suggested circuitry. Remo saw junctures at several spots. The hands were encased in what Remo saw were white gloves, and the feet in white boots. Remo noticed that the boots had unusually thick soles. The creature appeared to be about five-foot-five—but three inches of that was boot sole.

Then Remo noticed a rheostat on the thing's lower stomach. About where a belt buckle would be. Remo blinked. It *was* attached to a belt after all. A white one. For some reason, the belt's edges were indistinct, just like the outlines of the creature. It all blended in.

"Chiun, look at him closer. Do you have trouble with your eyes?"

"My eyes are perfect," Chiun snapped. But when he stared at the creature, he had to look away. He batted his hazel eyes and looked again.

"This creature is attempting to trick my eyes," Chiun said, kicking at it again.

"Hmmmm," Remo said. He put his hand over the thing's face. The head retreated a little, but only a little. Remo passed his hands up and down before the blister, testing it. The blank face moved up and down, following Remo's gestures.

"I think it can see us."

"Of course," Chiun said testily. "It is not blind. How could it know to hide within a tree if it could not see?"

"But it doesn't have any face—that I can see," Remo added. He looked at the head more closely.

"Do not bother me with trivial details," Chiun spat. He puffed out his cheeks and blew gusty breaths at the creature, as if trying to blow out a candle. His mighty efforts made his face redden, but otherwise had no effect.

Remo stared. The blister was opaque. He could not see into it. He wondered what the thing thought it was doing by just standing there. Before, it had run. Was it taunting them now? Remo pretended to draw back, but on a hunch, sent his fist crashing for the face.

The creature quailed as if struck a mortal blow. But it shook its head and resumed its defiant stance.

Remo took Chiun aside.

"We can see it. But we can't touch it."

"There is no scent either."

"Look, I know it seems spooky, but I don't think it's a ghost."

"Of course it is not a ghost. Remo, do not be ridiculous. Ghosts do not look like that thing. It is electrical."

"That's my conclusion. So what do we do?"

"Let us attempt to communicate with it," Chiun said, girding his kimono skirts and marching back to the waiting creature.

"Why don't you let me try?" Remo offered. "You're pretty upset, I can tell."

"Can you speak fluent Russian?"

"You know I can't."

"Then this is my task. For I speak excellent Russian, as does this creature."

"How do you know that?"

"The word it spoke on two occasions," Chiun said. "*Krahseevah*. It is Russian for 'beautiful.' "

"Beautiful? Beautiful what?"

"Simply 'beautiful.' Like a sunset or an Ung poem. It is an exclamation of appreciation."

As they approached the creature, a red light suddenly glowed in the center of its belt rheostat. It lit up like a resentful red eye.

The creature looked down. It started. Abruptly it

turned and clumped off stiff-leggedly. It waved its arms as if on fire.

"Come on," Remo shouted.

They overhauled the creature easily. They kept pace with it. Every so often, Chiun reached out in a futile attempt to grab it. Remo simply kept pace. The bulbous face continually bent down to the glow from the rheostat buckle.

"I got a hunch about this," Remo called.

The creature dodged toward a stand of trees by the side of a road.

"Damn," Remo said. "Once he's in those trees, he's going to pull one of those vanishing acts of his."

"If you are so concerned about that," Chiun said querulously, "then you attempt to stop him. I am the one doing all the work."

"Where the hell is Robin, I wonder?" Remo asked, looking over his shoulder.

He saw the helicopter almost as soon as he heard the *wop-wop-wop* of its rotor. It was Robin. She was bearing down on them, the chopper's skids skimming the nap of the ground.

"Don't look now, Chiun, but Robin's got her feathers in an uproar," Remo shouted. "Better duck!"

Remo hit the ground. Chiun danced out of the way as the helicopter, twisting like an angry wasp, swept overhead. It went through the running creature and lifted just clear of the trees.

When it circled back, there was no sign of the creature. There was only the shadow-clotted stand of trees.

The helicopter circled angrily. Then, as if relenting, it settled to the ground.

"It's in that bunch of trees," Remo said, opening the door.

Robin sat staring through the Plexiglas bubble.

"Robin?"

"I went right through him," she choked. "He went through me. I didn't feel anything. He was inside this helicopter. Then he was gone. It was like he wasn't real."

"Why don't you just come out?" Remo said solicitously. "We'll talk about it."

He reached out to take her arm. She wouldn't budge.

"He is a ghost, isn't he? An actual ghost."

"No," Remo said. "He's no ghost. Come on out and I'll try to explain it to you."

"I never used to believe in ghosts," Robin said in a stunned voice. "They didn't fit into my world. They're not in the regs."

8

When Robin Green was collected enough to step from the Bell Ranger helicopter, Remo patiently explained what he and Chiun had witnessed.

"So you see," Remo finished quietly, "he can't be a ghost. Ghosts don't run around with battery packs strapped to their backs."

Robin shuddered visibly. "I went *through* him," she moaned. "It was as if he was laughing at me. And that unnatural white face!"

"All white faces are unnatural," Chiun said under his breath. He was staring into the silent trees.

"Do you mind?" Remo said. Turning to Robin again, he took her by the shoulders. He looked her square in the eye. "Come on, get a grip on yourself. That was no ghost. Just because we can't explain it doesn't mean we have to be afraid of it."

Robin looked up. Her blue eyes were miserable.

"I don't know how to feel about this anymore," she said, her voice hollow. Her lower lip trembled uncontrollably.

"Join the club. But if we're going to deal with this, we're going to have to do it rationally. Even Chiun doesn't believe it's a ghost anymore. He says it's Russian."

"Russian?" Robin said sharply.

"That word, *krahseevah*," Remo explained. "It's Russian. It means 'beautiful.' "

"He said that when he saw the jeans," Robin said
slowly. "And the steaks."

"Then he is definitely a Russian," Chiun announced.
"Only a Russian would become excited over American blue jeans." He kept his narrow eyes on the trees.

"Hah! There! Did you see?" he demanded, pointing.

Remo's head snapped around. He saw a ghostly white
light slip between two trees.

"Okay," Remo said decisively. "He's on the move
again. My guess is he'll try to confuse us with the old
shell game. Instead of which shell is the pea under,
it'll be which tree is the *Krahseevah* hiding in."

"*Krahseevah?*" Chiun and Robin said in unison.

"Anybody got a better name for it?" Remo wanted
to know.

No one did. Swiftly Remo explained his plan.

"Robin. You get up in the air. I think our *Krahseevah*
is in trouble. Chiun and I will try to flush him out of
the trees. See if you can spot him when he tries to
leave. When you get a fix, we'll just hop on and follow
him."

"What good will that do?" Robin asked doubtfully.
"You know we can't touch him. How can we catch
him?"

Remo kept an eye on the tree the *Krahseevah* had
entered as he answered. "It's like this," he said. "It
knows we can't touch it, yet when we chased it, it
stopped dead and let us prove that for ourselves. It
could have kept on going. But I think it wanted to
discourage us. Maybe it figured if we realized it was
beyond our reach, we wouldn't bother to follow it."

"It is protecting something," Chiun said quickly. "A
lair, perhaps."

"Exactly," Remo returned. "And if it's trying to get
to a special place, maybe we can trap it there.
Somehow."

"A sound plan," Chiun said. "Let us execute it."

"Are you with us on this?" Remo asked Robin.

Robin Green stuck out her chin decisively. "I'm going to clip this bird's wings," she said. "You just watch me."

She ran to the helicopter and sent it into the air. She circled methodically.

Remo turned to Chiun. "Okay, know which tree he went behind?"

"Of course."

"Good. Go for it. I'll circle in from the other side. I have a hunch he won't stay inside very long. Maybe he can't. Let's see what develops."

Remo slipped around the edge of the stand. Then he plunged in. He moved quietly, making less sound than a stalking cat. His deep-set brown eyes adjusted to what was now pitch blackness. He would not need his night vision to spot the glowing *Krahseevah*, but it helped to avoid ground roots and rocks. The *Krahseevah* might be as stealthy as Sinanju, but Remo guessed it could hear, even if it didn't have external ears.

He came up on a great box elder. Chiun stood guard over it.

Chiun laid a finger to his lips as a signal for Remo to be silent.

Remo nodded. He pointed to the tree. Chiun nodded firmly.

They waited. After ten minutes, Remo began to have doubts. His idea was to surround the tree so they were ready when the thing made its next move. He looked around. He picked a fortunate time to look around. About thirty yards distant, a faint glow appeared on the trunk of a great elm. It was like a luminous fungus.

"Over there," Remo said, waving Chiun along.

The luminous spot quickly withdrew.

When they got to the tree, they surrounded it.

"What did you see?" Chiun demanded hotly.

"It stuck its face out of the bark," Remo whispered. "Right . . . about . . . here." He tapped the spot.

Chiun peered intently. "You are certain?"

"One way to find out."

It was a relatively old tree, so Remo simply attacked it with the hard edge of his hand. He hammered away, each blow splitting off chunks of bark and pale wood.

The trunk keeled over with splintering finality. Remo was set to react instantly to what was revealed. To his surprise, there was only emptiness where the elm had stood.

"Damn!" Remo said. "He must have slipped out the back."

Chiun's eyes raked the surroundings. "That one," he announced. He flounced to a nearby oak. He approached it angrily. With a single fingernail he split the trunk down the center. It separated, falling in two equal halves.

But the *Krahseevah* was not inside that tree either.

"Now what do we do?" Remo asked, looking around at the ranks of trees. "We can't chop them all down."

"Why not?" Chiun demanded, attacking another oak. It fell with a thunderclap of sound.

"Because that farmer we met probably owns this grove. Probably makes his living off them. Farmers have it tough enough these days. Hey! Over there," Remo suddenly spat out.

They saw the *Krahseevah* slip between two distant trees like a will-o'-the-wisp. It melted into an oak.

They attacked the oak with furious energy. It was dying, the roots and limbs rotten. Their blows shook it, but the wood was soft—so soft that the oak simply shed chips instead of toppling. It took them nearly five minutes of hand-and-foot chipping to reduce the dying tree to a ragged broken stump.

Still no *Krahseevah*.

"This could go on all night," Remo groaned.

"Better that we split up," Chiun suggested. "We will have a greater chance of finding it."

They went their separate ways. Above their heads,

Robin's helicopter circled and circled. Then the rotor sound began to miss and sputter.

"Uh-oh," Remo said. He went up an elm and watched as the helicopter settled to earth. Robin flew out of it. She fell to kicking the helicopter's snout in frustration.

"Everyone's in a bad mood tonight," he said, coming down from the branches.

When Robin Green got tired of abusing the helicopter, she approached the trees. Remo glided up behind her.

"Boo!" he said gently.

She turned on him, her face angry. "Don't do that!"

"Sorry. Run out of gas?"

Robin nodded. "I radioed for a jeep. We're not licked yet."

"Let's hope. We spotted it a bunch of times. But it's slippery."

"They're bringing chain saws too."

"Don't you think you're taking this to extremes? Somebody went to a lot of trouble to plant these trees a long time before we were born."

"A tree is just a tree. But national security is forever. Besides, this is just a shelterbelt. It's here to keep snowdrifts off the silo-access roads."

"Just so I'm not the one being sued. Let's go find Chiun."

They found Chiun stalking the shelterbelt like an angry tiger. He was not happy, and looked it.

"I think the Russian is gone," Chiun said sourly.

"What makes you say that, Little Father?" Remo asked.

"I have kept a sharp watch. I have seen no glowing lights. I think he has left this place."

"If he has, then we've really lost him," Robin said morosely.

"Might as well wait for the jeep," Remo ventured. "We're not going anyplace without it."

When the jeep pulled up, driven by an SP wearing fatigues and a blue beret, Robin Green ran to meet it. She rooted around in the back and then glared in the driver's freckled face.

"What's this?" she shouted, pointing back. "One miserable chain saw?"

"It's all I could find," the SP said. "The Air Force doesn't fight many forests."

"Watch your mouth, airman," Robin snapped, yanking the chain saw up onto her shoulder.

"Go easy on him," Remo said. "He's just trying to help. And what happened to the scared little girl of a few minutes ago?"

"I was not scared," Robin insisted. "I was thrown off my stride."

"Whatever. Look, as I said before, we're not going to get anywhere running in all directions at once and screaming at the top of our lungs. Forget the chain saw. It would take all night to cut every one of these trees down. And I think Chiun is right. It slipped away. Once we lost the helicopter, it must have known it could make a break for it unseen. It did. Let's try to pick up the trail."

"Where, genius? Where do we start?"

"Yes, genius," Chiun inserted. "Where should we start? It is a large state."

Remo turned to the driver. "Buddy, where's the nearest gas station?"

"Civilization or Mogas?"

"What's Mogas?"

"Military gas depot. We got one at Grand Forks."

"He wouldn't go there," Remo mused aloud. "Civilization."

"About five miles north of here."

"Good," Remo said, hopping into the passenger seat. "Take us there."

When Robin and Chiun hesitated, Remo said, "Shake a leg. We haven't got all night."

They piled in the back. Chiun threw the chain saw over the side, claiming that he needed to make room for himself, but actually he wanted to get rid of the detested smell of oil.

"Why, pray tell, are we going to a gas station?" Robin asked as they flew down the road.

"Yes, Remo. Pray tell, why?" Chiun demanded.

"How did you end up on her side?" Remo asked Chiun. "Never mind. Look, the *Krahseevah* acted pretty cocky when we first cornered it. Then that red light went on and it took off like it had ants in its pants. I think that light meant that its battery was going. My guess is that it's going to get it recharged."

"Oh, that's absurd," Robin snorted.

"You have a better theory?"

Robin lapsed into sullen silence. The rushing air threw her red hair around as the jeep sped through the empty North Dakota night.

They pulled up at Ed's Filling Station. It was a tar-paper shack with two old-fashioned pumps set in the dirt. One pump was regular, the other gave unleaded, Ed, the proprietor, said.

"But the unleaded one ain't working," he added.

"Never mind the gas," Remo shot back. "See anything of a guy in white coveralls?"

"You mean the Russian?"

"Russian?" Remo, Chiun, and Robin said in the same flat blank voice.

"Yup. Leastways, he sounded Russian to me. I never met a Russian before, but he had the accent. You know, like they do on the TV."

"Let me guess," Remo said. "He bought a battery?"

"Good guess," Ed said. "But no. We don't sell batteries here. Just gas. He said his car broke down a ways back. Battery went dead. Needed a recharge. Smart guy. He had it slung on his back."

"And you gave it to him!" Robin shouted in an accusing voice.

"What else was I gonna do? Stranded motorist like that. Of course I did. Fixed him up real good."

"You didn't notice that he was dressed rather oddly, did you?" Robin asked, arching an eyebrow.

"You mean the plastic suit? Sure, he looked kinda like an astronaut. He even carried a helmet under his arm. I thought it strange, all right. Why would he carry his helmet all this way? No one's gonna steal it from his car, way out here."

"You saw his face?" Robin asked. "What did he look like?"

Ed considered. "Nothing special about him. Friendly. Kinda on the dark side. Black hair, black eyes. Your basic Russian type, I'd say."

"And you're obviously such an expert." Robin sneered.

"Let's cut to the chase," Remo interrupted. "Which way?"

"Well, he came from that direction," Ed stated, pointing south. "But when he was done, he took off in that direction." Ed pointed north. "After he made the call, that is."

"Call?" Remo asked.

"Yeah, asked to use my pay phone. Said sure. No harm in it that I could see. He called a cab."

"Happen to remember the name of the cab company?" Remo said, pulling out a twenty-dollar bill. "It would mean a lot to us."

"Keep your twenty. I don't need it. I'm the only gas station for forty miles hereabouts. I do fine. Why do you think I can afford not to stock batteries?"

"So which one?" Remo asked, pocketing the twenty.

"Ned's Cab. We don't have no real cab companies out here. Ned's the only hired driver you can get."

"Got his number?"

"Business card's taped to the pay phone. See for yourself."

"Great," Remo said, hopping out of the jeep. "Thanks."

Remo went to the pay phone. He dialed Ned's Cab. Ned himself answered.

"You picked up a Russian at Ed's Filling Station," Remo said. "Do you remember where you took him?"

"He wasn't no Russian," Ned insisted. "Told me he was a Czech."

Remo sighed. "Did he wear a white coverall suit?"

"That's the one."

"Now we're getting someplace. Where'd you take him?"

"I dropped him off at the Holiday Inn on Interstate Twenty-nine."

"Great. Appreciate it."

When Remo rejoined the others, Ed asked, "Ned help you out?"

"He did. Thanks," Remo told him.

"Good. Because if he didn't, I woulda boxed his ears. Ned's my twin brother."

"Thanks," Remo said as he climbed back into the jeep. He nodded to the driver and they drove off, Ed waving an oily rag in farewell.

As they tore along the road, the sun came up, turning the distant sky orange.

"He was dropped off at a Holiday Inn," Remo told the driver. "Know it?"

"Sure. All the local hookers work out of that one."

"Good. Take us there."

"You don't think you'll actually find him there, do you?" Robin demanded. "Wouldn't he have switched to a car or another cab?"

"One halting step at a time," Remo said.

The desk clerk was extremely helpful. He told them that he would have to speak to the manager before he could answer any questions about the hotel's guests.

Robin Green, putting on a charming if strained smile, leaned over the desk and whispered something low and breathy.

The clerk leaned forward, his brows growing together as he concentrated. His eyes fell to Robin's ample chest.

"I didn't quite catch that, miss," he began.

Then Robin yanked his face down onto the shiny countertop and stuck a cocked automatic in his left ear.

"I said if you're hard of hearing, I got just the thing to clean the wax out of your ears," she shouted.

The desk clerk looked to Remo with wild, pleading eyes.

"I'd answer her," Remo said seriously. "She's been like that all day." He smiled. The clerk's face sagged like hot taffy

"Foreign accent? White coveralls?" he said quickly. "Room 5-C. Been here two weeks. He's registered as Ivan Grozny."

"Thank you," Robin said politely, releasing the desk clerk. "You've been very helpful. Anything else you care to tell us?"

"The elevator's around the corner."

They started for the elevator. Remo paused to have a word with the desk clerk. "If you're thinking of giving the room a buzz to warn anyone, don't. We know where you work."

"My break starts in five minutes."

"Why not get a head start on it?" Remo suggested pleasantly. "You probably don't want to be on duty when the fun starts."

They exited the elevator on the fifth floor. Remo led them to the room marked 5-C. He waved for them to stay back, and slipped under the door peephole. No sense in taking any chances.

Remo put his ear to the door. He heard the unmistakable beeping of a Touch-Tone telephone at work. Good, Remo thought. He's preoccupied. Remo got down on the garish red-and-blue rug and tried to peer under the crack in the door. He was in luck. He saw the legs of assorted furniture. And near a circular lampstand stood a pair of white plastic boots. They were sharp and clear this time. Not fuzzy-looking at all. And they didn't glow.

Remo took that as a good sign. He eased himself to his feet and joined the others.

"He's making a call," Remo told them. "This is perfect. Chiun and I will go first. You stay back until we subdue him. If we can."

"Try to stop me!" Robin said, waving her automatic.

Remo calmly relieved Robin of her weapon. He held it up and shoved his index finger down the barrel. The mechanism cracked. The slide fell off.

"I meant it," Remo warned, leaving Robin to stare at her maimed weapon in wonderment.

"Ready, Chiun?" Remo asked. They placed themselves on either side of the door. Chiun nodded silently.

"Okay," Remo said. "One . . . two . . . three!"

Remo cracked the lock with a short-armed blow while Chiun pulverized the hinge-supporting wood with hammerlike blows. The door felt in like a ramp.

They jumped in. And stopped dead in their tracks.

The room was empty. The telephone receiver dropped to the rug with a soft thud.

"Damn!" Remo snapped. "He's made his move. Search everywhere."

Chiun pulled open the bathroom door. It was empty. Remo checked the closet. Also empty. They looked out the window. The parking lot was deserted.

Remo lunged into the corridor. "He slipped through one of the walls," he shouted. "Knock on every door. Someone must have seen him. You, airman. Call the front desk. Keep an open line. I want to know if he tries to escape through the lobby."

Remo knocked on the next room. Getting no answer, he forced it. The room was dark. Deserted. He hurried to the next room. A sleepy man answered.

"See anything of a man in white?" Remo asked

earnestly. "With no face? We think he might have walked through your walls."

The door slammed in Remo's face and the guest could be heard angrily complaining to the front desk.

Working her way down the corridor, Robin knocked on doors. She was propositioned twice and had to slap one man who refused to take no for an answer.

They rendezvoused near the elevator.

"No sign of him," the SP reported. "Nobody fits the description the gas-station owner gave us. And he wasn't seen in the lobby."

"Then he's gotta be on this floor," Remo offered.

"Maybe he's a master of disguise," Robin suggested.

At the end of a half-hour they had marched every hotel guest out of his or her room.

"Repeat after me," Chiun was telling them. *"Krahseevah."*

"Krahseevah," they recited. Or those who remained conscious did.

"No, one at a time," Chiun said. "I wish to hear your accents."

One by one, the fifth-floor guests repeated the word *krahseevah* in accents ranging from a mellow Californian warble to a midwestern twang.

"None of them is Russian," Chiun decided.

"Maybe he's a voice mimic," Remo suggested.

"We're wasting our time," Robin insisted. "He got away. Maybe down the stairs or the elevator."

"No, at least one of us was in the hallway at all times. He couldn't have taken the stairs or the elevator."

"But he's not on this floor. Unless . . . unless he's inside one of the walls."

"Then we will tear down every treasonous wall until we uncover the culprit," Chiun announced, to the horror of everyone, including Remo.

"What do you think?" Remo asked Robin.

"We gotta get this guy. Let's do it!"

*   *   *

When the lobby switchboard lit up with frightened calls that the fifth floor was being systematically dismantled by maniacs, the police were called. Two patrolmen entered from the elevator with their service revolvers drawn.

Robin met them with a hard face and a resolute tone of voice.

"We have a report of a disturbance on this floor," one of the cops said in a dead monotone.

"Green, OSI," she said, flashing her ID. "We're confiscating this floor in the name of national security."

The cops hesitated. They examined her ID card carefully. Then they eyed her up and down, lingering wistfully on her bustline, which strained at her uniform blouse.

Finally they handed the card back to her. "Sounds like the hotel is being dismantled," one of them said while the other stared up and down the corridor.

"Just the walls on this floor," Robin said crisply. "We're looking for stolen military equipment we believe to be hidden in the walls."

The cops hesitated and went off into a corner to confer.

Finally they said, "We'll have to check with our superiors."

"Have them call Grand Forks AFB. But do it from the lobby. This floor is off-limits to civilians."

The police reluctantly departed. Robin found Remo and explained the situation to him.

Remo was tearing crumbling plaster chunks from the room the *Krahseevah* had occuped. "Can you really confiscate a hotel?" he asked, his hand crushing plaster like a jackhammer. "A tree I can understand. But an entire hotel?"

"It's just this floor. And between you and me, I have no idea what my jurisdictional limits are in a situation like this. I just want this guy any way I can nail him."

"Well, I have *some* good news for you," Remo said. "Check out the closet."

Robin looked. On the floor of the closet was a heap covered by a sheet. Under the sheet was an assortment of circuit boards and other mechanical devices, two pairs of Calvin Klein blue jeans, and a Styrofoam cooler crammed with porterhouse steaks.

"Bingo!" Robin Green said. "Now all we need is the thief himself."

But they turned up no trace of the *Krahseevah*. They finally gave up after reducing the inner walls of the fifth floor to skeletal supports. Chiun suggested that the outer wall be demolished too. But Remo prevailed upon him that those walls were too thin to contain a human being, and besides the hotel might collapse. Chiun reluctantly concurred.

"He's done it again," Robin said as they stood in the room they had chased the *Krahseevah* to. "Now what?"

Remo happened to notice the telephone receiver. It was lying on the floor where the *Krahseevah* had dropped it when they surprised him.

"He was making a call," Remo said. "Let's see if he completed it. Might lead us somewhere."

"What if he was just sending out for Chinese?" Robin asked.

"Let's not sink into total despair. We haven't done too badly so far."

Robin Green looked around the fifth floor. It was a shambles in which identical furniture arrangements surrounded them like some Daliesque repeating image.

"I wish to God I knew how I'm going to explain this," she said weakly. "I'll have to write a report as thick as the Yellow Pages."

9

Down in the lobby, Remo asked the switchboard operator if she had any record of an outgoing call from room 5-C.

Even though Remo did his best to be polite, the operator quailed from him as if from a polar bear lumbering into her cubicle. It was the plaster dust on his face and hair that frightened her. She had fielded the frenzy of calls during the early-morning hours when it looked as if the hotel was about to come crashing down.

"One . . . one moment," she said jerkily. She called up a file on her terminal screen.

"One call was made at five-oh-two," she told him. "It lasted less than a minute."

"What's the number?" Remo asked.

"It's this one," she said, placing a trembling pink-painted nail on a line of green glowing digits.

Remo memorized the number.

"Okay. Now get me an outside line."

When the operator handed him her headset, Remo took her by one elbow and eased her out of her chair.

"This is private," he said gently but firmly. "Take a coffee break. I won't be long."

Remo dialed a number. It rang a chiropractor's office in Santa Ana, California, and then was routed through the switchboard of radio station KDAD in

nearby Riverside, finally ringing a phone on the desk
of Dr. Harold W. Smith in Folcroft Sanitarium, the
cover for CURE.

"Smith? Remo here. We're making progress. I don't
have time to explain it all right now, and maybe you
wouldn't believe me if I did, but we traced the thief to
a Holiday Inn. Recovered some of the stuff he filched.
But he slipped away.'"

"Where?" Smith's lemony voice inquired.

"Into the Twilight Zone, for all I know. Look, it's
complicated. I'll fill you in later. Just trust me. Here's
a phone number. Can you tell me who he was calling?
It's our only lead."

"One moment, Remo," Smith said.

At Folcroft, Smith called up the reverse telephone
directory data base. It was an electronic version of a
telephone-company publication few knew existed. It
listed all phone numbers in numerical order by region,
cross-referencing each one to the subscriber's name
and address.

Smith keyed in the area code—which he recognized
as Washington, D.C.—then the exchange, and finally
the last four digits.

"Oh, my God," he said hoarsely, staring at the
answer.

"Yeah? What've you got?" Remo asked.

"It's the Soviet embassy in Washington."

"Great! It fits, Smitty. The thief spoke Russian."

"He did? Remo, if the Soviets have been systematically looting LCF-Fox, there's no telling how much
damage they could do—have already done."

"Maybe it's time Chiun and I paid a courtesy call on
the embassy," Remo suggested.

"No. Don't. Things are bad enough. This could
escalate into a major diplomatic incident. This re-
quires careful planning. If the trail is cold, you will
both return to Folcroft for debriefing at once. I will
decide how to proceed once I speak with the President."

"You're the boss, Smitty. See you soon."

By the time Remo left the switchboard desk, the lobby was filled with local police officers and a contingent of high-ranking Air Force officers and SP's from Grand Forks Air Force Base.

Robin Green was excitedly attempting to explain the ruined state of the fifth floor.

"I'm telling you," she flung at them, "I didn't steal any of that stuff. It was the Russian. And he's probably hiding inside one of these walls laughing at us. But you turkeys are so afraid of lawsuits you won't check it out."

Chiun stood back from the tight knot of uniforms, his face as innocent as a child's.

Remo sidled up to him. "What's going on?"

"They are badgering that poor girl," Chiun told him.

"They're going to want to talk to us next," Remo said. "And Smith is recalling us to Folcroft. Let's slip out the back."

"Oh, they will not bother us. I have already told them I do not even know that poor unfortunate girl whose ravings are plainly the product of a deranged mind."

"You said that?"

"Of course. How could I keep Emperor Smith waiting?"

"But you didn't know that Smith wanted us back until I told you just now."

"Nonsense," Chiun said as they slipped out a fire exit. "I knew you were calling Smith and I knew Smith would call us home. For what else can we do here?"

"I wish there was something we could do to help Robin," Remo said as they got to the waiting jeep.

"I am sure they will find a nice quiet place for her to rest in," Chiun said.

"That's what I'm afraid of," Remo muttered as he

sent the jeep out of the parking area. "Still, that voice does get on the nerves after a while, doesn't it?"

Chiun nodded. He idly picked up a leaf that had blown onto his lap and held it up to the wind. The wind tore it away. "She complains too much," he sniffed.

Remo gave Chiun a sidelong skeptical glance and shook his head slowly.

10

Captain Rair Brashnikov knew he was dead.

All the signs were there. He felt light, disembodied, and he was moving through a dark tunnel at incredible speed. He swished. It was exactly as his grandfather, Illya Nicolaivitch Brashnikov, had once described it to him back in Georgia, USSR, when he was a boy.

Grandfather Brashnikov had been driving his ancient Ford tractor when he suffered a heart attack. He was still sitting in the hard seat, his face slate blue, when the front tire bumped a rock and tipped over. Rair's father was the first on the scene. He had tried reviving his father with artificial respiration, and when that didn't change the blue-turning-gray color of his face, he pounded on his father's chest in frustration.

It was the pounding that did the trick. Grandfather Brashnikov coughed up phlegm and was carried hacking and spitting to the family house, adjacent to the collective potato farm where they all toiled.

That night, over dinner, Grandfather Brashnikov described his experience.

"I was in vast tunnel," he explained, a joyful gleam in his old eyes. "Beyond tunnel were stars, the most scintillating stars ever imagined. I felt myself being hurled through tunnel toward wonderful clean light. That is only word I know to describe this light. It was silvery. Pure.

"Then," he went on, "I felt myself slow down. Something tugged me back. I did not want to leave light. I was dead. I knew it in my heart. I was dead and yet I did not fear death. I wanted to be with light. I think"—he lowered his voice and fixed Rair with his renewed eyes—"I think this light was God."

"No one believes in God anymore, *dedushka*," Rair had said. He was fourteen and thought he knew more than his seventy-year-old grandfather.

"Hush, Kroshka," he said, using a nickname—"Crumb"—Grandfather Brashnikov used when he wished to remind Rair that he had once played on his grandfather's knee. "Let me finish my story. I felt myself drawn back. The light faded in the distance. When I opened my eyes once again, your father—my son—was beating on my chest." He laughed ruefully. "My ribs still ache. I am happy to be with family, but I feel sad too. For I ache for that light the way I used to ache for my dead wife, Saint Basil preserve her."

Rair never forgot the story of his grandfather, who lived another ten years but came away from being dead with a lighter step and joy-filled heart. He was a man who had faced death and found it an experience filled with hope, not gloom.

The dark walls of the tunnel flew past Rair. He looked to see his body, but he had none. He was part of the darkness. He looked ahead of him, seeking the pure clean light that had once stirred his grandfather's soul. But he saw nothing like it. Only the snaking, whizzing walls of the tunnel through which he passed, no more substantial than a beam of light himself.

So this was death, Rair thought. It was not so bad. Certainly preferable to facing a KGB firing squad, which had nearly been his fate.

As he raced along, Rair Brashnikov reflected on the events that had brought him to his death.

Had it started when he joined the KGB as a signals intelligence analyst? Or before that, the first time he

felt that urge which was to dominate his life and nearly
end his career at the age of thirty-one? Or had it truly
begun the day they came to cell number twenty-six in
the basement of Moscow's Lefortovo Prison. His cell.

It was cold in Lefortovo. For a prison that had
known many famous occupants, from survivors of the
czarist days to framed American journalists, it was
unremarkable. A stone cell with a blue steel cot and
scratchy camel-hair blankets.

Rair Brashnikov had spent less than two months in
that cell, shunned except for the daily portion of runny
soup and a mashed-potato-and-fish mixture in a cracked
bowl shoved through the feed window of the rust-
colored door.

Then one day they came for him.

They were two corporals and the prison's commandant. One of the corporals opened the cell with a
grating brass key.

Rair Brashnikov cowered in his bunk. It was too
soon. They had come for him too soon.

"*Nyet.* Not today. I do not want to die today," he
whimpered, pulling the coarse blanket over his head.

"Come with us, thief," said the commandant. "Do
not be a woman."

He was hauled out of the cell by the corporals, set
on his feet, and handed his soft gray slippers. The men
towered over Brashnikov, who had barely met the
KGB's minimum-height requirement. He had the nimble body of a ballet dancer.

It was the middle of the night, which puzzled
Brashnikov. Usually they shot prisoners at dawn. Of
course KGB firing squads were normally reserved for
captured spies, not cashiered KGB intelligence captains like himself.

Instead, snapping their fingers as a warning to the
guards that a prisoner was being transferred, they
escorted him to a garage and put him blindfolded into
a car. Minutes later he found himself in a heavily

guarded office. It was the office of the general who
ran the KGB. Semoyan. He was in KGB headquarters.

"Leave him," General Semoyan had said. His face
was a dour mask. "Sit."

Rair Brashnikov took the hard wooden chair the
general indicated with a careless wave.

"You are thief, Rair Brashnikov," General Semoyan
said. His voice was matter-of-fact, not accusing.

"Da," Rair had admitted. His eyes leapt to the general's T-shaped desk. There was a gold pen in a holder.
Rair wondered if it was solid gold or merely gilt.

"You have been convicted of stealing KGB office
supplies and selling them on black market."

"I cannot help myself," Rair blurted out. "I have
had this urge since I was boy."

"Do not make excuses, Tovarich Brashnikov. I am
told you are very clever thief, if such a thing can be
said of a man who steals from his motherland and his
comrades in uniform."

"I will never do it again," Rair promised, leaping to
his feet. He leaned on the general's desk. His eyes
welled up with tears.

"I believe you," said General Semoyan. "Now, sit
down. Please."

"Thank you," said Rair Brashnikov, palming the
general's pen from its onyx holder. The pen felt heavy.
Yes, true gold. Rair slipped the pen up his frayed
cotton sleeve.

"We are prepared to reinstate you, comrade," the
general continued, "at your former rank of captain,
with all back pay and benefits. Your past crimes will
be expunged from your record."

"For that I will do anything," Rair promised. He
wrung his hands so the pen would not fall out. "Just
name the thing."

"You will go to USA."

"America?" Rair Brashnikov's voice had been filled
with disbelief. The general misinterpreted this as fright.

"You will be protected while you are between missions," General Semoyan assured him.

"America," Rair repeated. His mind was racing. The best electronic equipment came from America. The finest blue jeans. The food was incredible in its diversity. Red meat, it was said, was actually red in America. Not gray like Soviet gristle steaks.

The general's voice broke into his reverie. "If you fear it so, we can find another agent."

"*Nyet!*" said Rair Brashnikov. "I will undertake this mission. Just tell me what to do."

General Semoyan stood up. "Then come with me, Captain Brashnikov."

They escorted him to a room where a uniform with captain's bars was waiting for him. He was allowed to dress once more in civilized clothing with warm leather shoes on his feet, and, his black hair wet with fragrant hair oil, Rair emerged from the dressing room, his black eyes shining like rosary beads. The general's gold pen was tucked into a regulation sock.

Under guard, with General Semoyan in the lead, restored Captain Rair Nicolaivitch Brashnikov was brought deep into the subterranean bowels of KGB headquarters in Dzershinsky Square.

They halted before a thick steel door while security guards manipulated a complicated electronic lock. Above the door, in Cyrillic lettering, was a large sign:

REVERSE ENGINEERING DIRECTORATE

Rair Brashnikov wondered what reverse engineering meant as he was led into an antiseptic white room. Men in white smocks stood like students around a workbench. The air was tinged with ozone.

"Step up to bench, please," General Semoyan said. The others crowded around under the unstable fluorescent lighting.

On the bench were two objects. They appeared to be identical.

"This is component of the rocket motor of our new

shuttle spaceplane," General Semoyan told Brashnikov, tapping one of them.

"It is quite . . . shiny," Rair ventured. In fact it was very shiny. Rair wondered what it might fetch on the black market. He shoved his hands into his trouser pockets. There were too many witnesses in this room. He could not palm it in full view of all these men.

The general hefted the other object.

"And this is component from American shuttle," he said. "Do they look similar to you?"

Rair took the second component in his hands and turned it over and over. The old urge tugged at his heart. Reluctantly he replaced it on the bench's grainy surface.

"Yes," he said firmly. "They are identical. A testament to the ability of Soviet technicians to match much-vaunted Americans."

"No," the general said. "A tribute to good fortune and what we call reverse engineering."

"I do not know this term, 'reverse engineering,' " Rair admitted. He wondered what this had to do with America.

"You understand principle of engineering a tool or machine part, *nyet*? One begins with prototype. From this, blueprint is made. And from blueprint, many copies are built. Here is blueprint of the rocket-motor part. See? It shows in exacting detail how the components are to be manufactured, how to machine fine thicknesses of parts and how to join parts together to result in a working mechanism."

"*Da*, I understand," said Brashnikov.

"No, you do not. While this Soviet component was built from Soviet blueprint, it is not total story. For these blueprints are not drawn from Soviet prototype. They were created from this American component. One of our agents obtained this from its point of manufacture. We took it apart, calibrated measurements and deduced materials, and developed blueprints. Thus, without incurring cost and time required to develop component that might or might not work properly first time, we have attained ability to mass-produce this part. Thus our shuttle soared as well as its American counterpart."

"Reverse engineering," Rair said blankly.

"Reverse engineering, *da*. For despite what you may have read in *Pravda* or *Izvestia* or whatever it is thieves read, Soviet technology still lags far behind the West. Even now, we have hundreds of agents in U.S. attempting to acquire working parts to everything from microwave ovens to neutron bombs."

"Whatever works," Rair said, inadvertently recoining an American catchphrase. He was trying to be diplomatic.

"But," General Semoyan went on, "even with all of our agents, America is too productive. Too creative. Often by the time a find comes into our hands and can be duplicated, it is already obsolete by Western standards. In short, we cannot steal American technology as fast as Americans can create and improve it."

"This is ironic," Rair said.

"This is tragic," the general countered. "For if this trend continues, we will be left far behind. Even now, almost seventy years after American society was first transformed by mass-produced automobile, Mother Russia still cannot build a decent affordable car."

Rair nodded unthinkingly. He drove a Lada.

General Semoyan laughed grimly. "Instead of making glorious revolution, we should have been making Model T's. And today, American computer technology is so far ahead of us, they will bury us in microchips. Khrushchev is no doubt turning in grave."

"I will be happy to steal as much American technology as you would like," Rair Brashnikov said bravely, "but I fear I am not equal to this mighty task."

"*Nyet*, you are not. No ordinary man is. But we can make you so. Bring it," the general said to a hovering technician.

The technician came back with a black box the size of a light traveling suitcase. It had a combination lock and two keyholes. The technician removed a small key from a chain around his throat and undid the locks. Then he worked the combination.

"What that man did, the unlocking, would defeat any thief," General Semoyan said coolly. "Even you, Brashnikov."

"Yes," Brashikov said, but he really meant "no." He was confident he could pick any lock. But he was afraid to seem like too much of a thief. He still couldn't take his eyes off the shiny shuttle components.

But when the technician opened the case and revealed a heap of white plastic, Brashnikov forgot all about the components.

"This," the general said proudly, "will allow you to defeat locks, doors, vaults, walls—even the most impregnable fortified military installations in USA."

The technician lifted the thing out of the case. It hung from his hands like a cosmonaut suit. Gloves and thick-soled boots lay in the case, along with what appeared to be a collapsed helmet. They were slick like plastic, but the skin was networked with pale plastic filaments.

"Please demonstrate our prize for Captain Brashnikov," General Semoyan ordered.

One of the technicans—the shortest of them—struggled into the suit. It took the help of two others to pull the skintight material on. It was like getting into a scuba suit that was a size too small. They sealed it in the back by Velcro flaps. The helmet went on the same way.

Rair noticed with interest that the face shield was not transparent glass or plastic, but a kind of opaque white cellophane. After the helmet was in place, the cellophane expanded. Then it contracted. Its rhythmic expansions were obviously the result of the technician's respiration.

"The facial membrane is like two-way mirror," General Semoyan explained as he noted Brashnikov's perplexed expression. "He can see out, but no one can see his face. It has added advantage of being permeable to oxygen, but proof against all known forms of chemical agents. However, its prime purpose is that no matter how well we train a man to prepare himself for rigors of wearing device, the human eye is designed to flinch from perceived obstacles, even when brain knows those obstacles cannot possibly harm it."

"I do not understand," Rair said as the technicans turned the man around. They hooked two white cables to ports on the suit's shoulders. The other ends were hooked up to an ordinary car battery. Then they fitted the battery into a webbed sling that attached to the man's back like a rucksack.

The man in the suit turned around and waited, his blank blister of a face crinkling as he breathed.

General Semoyan smiled expansively.

"If you are curious about the material, Captain Brashnikov, go ahead, touch it. Feel it if you wish."

Brashnikov touched the man's chest. It felt slick, like plastic. It was plastic, Rair decided, possibly some kind of rubberized plastic. The sewn-in tubes also felt plasticky. Fiberoptic cables, he decided.

"Does it feel solid to you?" the general asked pleasantly.

"Yes, of course. It is very substantial. Is it bulletproof?"

The general laughed loudly. "Yes," he said. "But not in the way you think. I mean, did it feel solid to the touch?"

"Yes," Rair said. What did the general mean? Of course it was solid. What else could it be?

"And this," General Semoyan asked, rapping on the bench. "Is it solid?"

Rair Brashnikov ran his fingers along the edges of the bench. He was careful to keep his fingers away from the shuttle parts which sat so carelessly, so temptingly within reach.

"Yes. It is oak."

"If you were to examine this table or that suit under an electron microscope, you would see that it is not as solid as it appears. For all matter in the universe is composed of atoms, all clustered together like the stars in the night sky."

"I know my science," Rair said defensively. "I have read of this."

"Then you doubtless understand that atoms are very, very tiny. And that they are protected by electrons whirling at speeds so high that they form protective shell like whirling blades of high-speed fan. And there are spaces between atoms as vast as void between stars."

"Yes."

"That table, that man, even you and I, are composed of vast empty spaces in which these tiny spheres cluster. You, when you are struck, you feel impact. You feel pain. Because these electrons protect empty spaces. From earth, stars in cosmos look to be mere inches apart, but we know that is not so. It is very opposite with atoms. We can see denseness which make them solid to touch, but not spaces between."

"I do not follow," Rair admitted.

"Then follow this." The general signed to the technician in the white plastic suit.

The technician reached down to his belt buckle. For the first time, Rair noticed a white rheostat on the buckle. The man turned it. Then, softly, the suit glowed.

Rair watched. His eyes hurt suddenly. He tried to focus them. But they wouldn't focus. The man seemed to blur at the edges. The veinlike network of filaments pulsed and ran with tiny golden lights. Even the webbing straps that held the battery pack in place grew indistinct.

Rair looked away. A blueprint on a wall was crystal clear. But when his gaze returned to the man in the suit, he couldn't quite focus on him.

"The effect you are trying to understand is result of hypervibration," General Semoyan announced. "Suit is vibrating at trillions of pulses per millisecond. This is why we have dubbed it our *zibriruyushchiy kostyum*, or vibration suit."

Rair walked around the man in the suit. There was something very odd about him now. Something he could not quite put his finger on.

When he looked closer at the man's concealed face, he recognized it. The featureless membrane expanded out like bubblegum bubble, but there was no crinkling sound anymore.

"If he spoke, we could not hear his voice, although he can understand us," the general explained.

"Will he become invisible?" Rair asked. Reasonably, he thought.

"That would be perfect, but no. You may touch him if you wish."

Rair hesitate. "Will it hurt?"

"*Nyet*, you will feel no pain. Nor will he."

Rair Brashnikov still held back. Why would they want him to touch the suit again? He reached out careful fingers. The tips of his fingers disappeared into it.

"Ahhh!" he cried, recoiling as if stung. "My hand!"

"Your hand is fine," General Semoyan assured him.

"I felt . . . nothing," Rair said in a dull incomprehending tone. He was pleased to see that he still had fingertips.

"Exactly," General Semoyan said. "It is much like known phenomenon of colliding galaxies. Astronomers know that in cosmos, galaxies sometimes collide. But there is no resulting catastrophe, for suns merely pass one another, so great are spaces between them. Vibration suit is vibrating so that its atomic structure is fluid, like water. When you place your hand within the field, suit compensates for your atomic structure. Its electrons are repelled by your electrons. The spaces merge, but atoms remain apart. Thus, your hand coexisted in the same physical space as his chest. At least, that is our theory."

"No bullet, no hand could harm him," Rair breathed, inching closer.

"No wall can stop him either." General Semoyan smiled. "Comrade, please demonstrate."

As Rair Brashnikov watched with wide black eyes, the man in the suit walked through the solid oak bench. He passed from it to one wall, walking as soundlessly as a ghost. He passed through the wall. Then he was gone. Utter silence filled the room as they stared at the blank white wall.

Soon the technician stepped from another wall. He emerged from it as if coming through a dense fog. Except he was the fog and the wall was solid.

"This is astonishing! This is incredible!" Rair Brashnikov shouted eagerly. "Who says Russian technology is backward? Who says we cannot compete with West? If Soviet science can produce such a wonder, there is nothing we cannot do!"

"We stole the suit from the Japanese," General Semoyan said dryly.

Rair subsided. "It is Japanese?"

"Another reason why you were chosen, captain. Aside from your criminal past, you are short and slim enough to fit into the suit. It was built by the Nishitsu Corporation, and is designed for the average Japanese male physique. We believe it is a by-product of their recent superconductor breakthroughs."

"You do not know?" Raid asked in surprise. "Why not take it apart and make blueprints, then build suit that will fit sturdy Russian?"

General Semoyan shook his leonine head.

"It is too complicated. We dare not dismantle it for fear of not being able to restore suit to proper operating order. Better to risk the suit in the field than to lose it to our incompetent technicians."

The technicians in the room shifted their feet and looked down in embarrassment.

General Semoyan cleared his throat. The technician in the suit turned it off. The blurry indistinctness of his outline faded with the lambent glow of the suit itself.

"We will train you to walk in suit," General Semoyan told him as the man was helped out of the suit, "to pass through solid objects without hesitation or fear. Then we will let you loose in America, with a shopping list of what we most need. Are you prepared for this, Captain Brashnikov?"

"As always, I am brave in the service of my motherland," Rair Brashnikov said, visions of American blue jeans and VCR's dancing in his head. He was so elated he did something he had never done since he picked his first pocket. He slipped the gold pen into the general's coat pocket.

That way, when Semoyan noticed it missing, even if he suspected Brashnikov, the proof of his innocence would eventually be found.

For Rair Brashnikov was not about to risk losing the opportunity to be set loose in the consumers' paradise of the world for a mere gold pen.

For months, they trained him. He learned that for all its wonders the vibration suit was fraught with hidden perils. One had to be careful how one walked. For the vibrations which allowed a man to pass through six feet of concrete would also cause him to sink into a floor.

The technicians who maintained it, obviously only dimly understood the suit. They explained to him that the thick boot soles contained tiny vibrating elements that caused the bottoms to vibrate in counterpoint to the suit vibration. Only a micron thickness of the bottom vibrated out of synchronization, they theorized. But it was enough to allow for footing and traction. Still, the suit wearer had to be careful, when he passed through an obstacle, that he did it with the toes and soles kept level.

Rair tried this a few times. It was a difficult skill to learn. If he stepped wrong, his upper body passed through the test walls, but his feet got hung up.

It took thirty days until he mastered the art of walking through a wall. At the same time, he had to deal with the eye's blinking reflex. The face membrane helped, but when a concrete wall came up to the eye, the eye naturally flinched and the body flinched too. Merely shutting the eyes was not enough. For Rair was taught that although he could pass through walls, he could not see through them. He could never be certain what was on the other side. It was imperative that before he dared enter such walls, he stick his face into them like a swimmer sticking his face above water to see what lay on the surface.

It took time, and skill, and it was difficult.

They taught him that he could trot while in the suit, but he could not run. Even with his body as insubstantial as smoke, his micron-thick soles could trip on ground rocks. If he tripped, he was told, he would fall. And if he fell . . .

"What?" Rair had asked anxiously.

The technician shrugged. They did not actually know, but they theorized that a fall would propel the suit through the earth's crust, where a man might, in theory, sink until he emerged on the opposite side of the globe.

"That would not be so terrible," Rair had said, visibly relieved.

True, they told him. But no one could say if, after passing through the earth, the man might not keep going, forever and ever, into deepest space.

"Oh," Rair had said in a sober voice.

There were other problems with the suit. The more he learned, the less he liked the assignment, but because giving up meant facing a firing squad, Rair Brashnikov continued training.

Even after they warned him that he must never, ever, turn off the suit while inside something solid.

"What would happen then?" he had asked fearfully.

On this the technicians were not in complete agreement.

One thought that Rair would become trapped like a fly in amber.

Another believed that the atomic structure of both substances would become inextricable, so that in his last moments Rair would taste wood or concrete in his mouth, his stomach would feel full of matter. His brain would be riddled with foreign nonorganic substances. His bodily fluids would mingle with the material. It would be a weird, terrible, suffocating death.

Still another theorized that with the vibration suit shut down, the repelling forces that kept the atoms separated would cease, possibly result in a nuclear explosion.

Rair Brashnikov kept the thought of becoming a walking Chernobyl in mind all through the Aeroflot flight from Moscow to Washington, D.C., where he met his case officer, the chargé d'affaires of the Soviet embassy, actually a KGB major. The chargé d'affaires provided Rair with a secure place to live between pentrations, which ranged from plucking key parts from U.S. missiles so that when they went awry and had to be destroyed, no one dreamed that they had malfunctioned because they had been pilfered, to obtaining mission-critical computer chips from Pentagon super-computers.

Through it all, Rair Brashnikov had been extra, extra careful not to be seen, not to be heard, not to be suspected. American security was so lax it was relatively easy. And Rair Brashnikov had been very, very well-trained. Even in America, the training continued. He was forced to enter mock-ups of cramped missile interiors, positioning himself so that when he deactivated the suit, no toe or finger remained inside anything solid. It was a simple matter, then, to remove whatever he wished, reactivate the suit, and slip away.

It was a happy property of the suit that whatever Brashnikov held in his hands when the suit activated, vibrated in sympathy so that it could be carried through solids as well.

Rair Brashnikov trained very hard. He did not desire to go up in a small mushroom cloud. Nor did he wish to be captured when the battery pack ran down, as it did when he was being pursued from LCF-Fox by the American with unusually thick wrists and the absurdly garbed Oriental.

The pair had been incredibly fleet of foot. And strong. They had chopped down a thick tree while he hid within. Rair had no idea who they were. He had been fascinated by them—until the rheostat warning light went on, indicating that he had only the sixty-minute reserve-energy supply left.

Rair had counted himself fortunate that he had so many trees to hide in. He had finally given them the slip, and made it back to his hotel, where he immediately reported his encounter with U.S. military personnel to the chargé d'affaires.

Rair had been certain that the trio had been left far behind. That had been a fatal mistake, he now realized.

As the dark tunnel walls zoomed past him, Brashnikov tried to remember his last moment of life. He had dialed the Soviet embassy. The switchboard had answered, and Rair had asked to speak with the chargé d'affaires, giving his code name, Lyovkiy Dukh—Nimble Ghost.

While he waited to be connected, the hotel-room door crashed in. Rair did not turn to see what had happened. That was not important. Turning on the suit was by then a reflex in any dangerous situation.

He remembered reaching for the belt rheostat. At the same time, the chargé d'affaire's voice came over the line, saying, "Hello?" That was the last thing Rair heard. The room went white like a star going nova, and now he was hurling through this endless tunnel at the speed of light.

The explanation was obvious. The suit must have gone nuclear. There was no other possible answer.

It had been the thing that Rair Brashnikov had most feared. Yet now that it had happened, he felt a curious lack of concern. It had been quick and painless. How much more could one expect from death?

And so Rair Brashnikov, only a little sad, rushed through the snaking tube, searching for the light his grandfather had spoken of so long ago, in another time and place.

It was a strange thing. In his ears, he could still hear the chargé d'affaires' angry voice. It kept repeating, "Hello? Hello? Are you there, Brashnikov? Answer me!"

And behind it, there were other voices. A multitude of them. Laughing and whispering. Shouting and sobbing. Rair thought they were the voices of the dead. If he listened hard enough, could he pick out his grandfather's voice too? he wondered.

But when he tried, he discovered a strange thing.

All the voices spoke English. American English.

How curious, Brashnikov thought. Were there no Soviets in the afterlife?

Then he heard the chargé d'affaires' voice again, angry and anxious, calling his name over and over again. It was most passing strange.

11

"It's okay, I'll get it," Remo Williams called out in response to the familiar knock. He leapt to the back door, swiping at the smoke that had seeped into the kitchen despite the insulation of two closed doors.

"Hi, Smitty," Remo said. "Back for more rice?" Then he stopped. "You look different. Did you break down and get a face lift?"

"Nonsense," Smith snapped, closing the door behind him like a nervous milkman on a dawn assignation.

"No, really," Remo returned, following him to the kitchen table. "There's something different about you. New haircut?"

"I have been using the same barber for nearly thirty years."

"And you probably tip him the same way you did in 1962."

"I consider my loyal patronage to be tip enough." Smith looked around, noticing the haze.

"Has someone been smoking?" he asked.

"Sort of. This is Chiun's latest kick."

Smith looked at Remo with disbelief. "I cannot imagine Chiun smoking."

"I'll explain later. I'm still trying to put my finger on what's different about you today. A new tie?" Remo asked. "No, that's a Dartmouth tie. And your suit the same. Gray as a mouse."

Smith took a seat at the table and laid a small brown carrying case on it.

Noticing this, Remo snapped his fingers.

"That's it!" he said. "That's not your usual brief-case. I *knew* you look different."

Smith looked at Remo as if uncertain if he was being kidded.

"Please sit down, Remo," he said quietly. Remo sat. He looked at the case. It was smaller than a suitcase, but larger than a valise. It was nearly a box. Remo wondered what was in it.

"Any leads on our missing spook?" Remo asked.

"None. I ran computer checks on all commerical and charter flights out of North Dakota. I don't be-lieve our man was on any of them. And the name he was registered under—Ivan Grozny—is fictitious. It means 'Ivan the Terrible.' We will have to pick up his trail when we can. Right now I have a more pressing task for you and Chiun."

"Did I hear my name spoken?" a squeaky voice said suddenly.

The Master of Sinanju suddenly stood in the now-open door. He wore a plain kimono. It was as white as a snowdrift, and it made the aged ivory texture of his wrinkled skin look actually brown.

Bluish smoke rolled around him like a fogbank.

"I was just starting to explain your next assign-ments," Smith said, his gray eyes alert to the excessive amount of smoke. He felt it tickle his throat and he coughed into his fist uncomfortably.

"Then I should be present to see that Remo does not misinterpret your precise instructions," Chiun remarked.

"I was just about to tell Remo that my computers have so far had no luck in tracing the creature you both encountered."

"What about his secret?" Chiun asked eagerly.

"It represents a technology beyond current knowledge," Smith admitted. "Although it is possible to assume the Russian—for surely the evidence points to a Soviet agent—wore an electronic suit that somehow enables him to pass through solids."

Chiun's face lost its hopeful expression. "Oh," he said. "I was hoping you, as a white familiar with machine techniques, could help me with my experiment."

"What experiment is that?" asked Smith.

"You'll be sorry you asked," Remo warned.

Chiun made low, furtive shooing motions at Remo.

"I have been attempting to duplicate this power, which no Master of Sinanju has ever possessed," Chiun said loftily.

"Really? I would like to see this."

Chiun stepped aside and bowed. "Enter."

Remo followed Smith into Chiun's personal room. The walls were covered with mirrors. They hung on the walls and leaned precariously against closet doors. Mirror tiles were neatly arranged on the floor and others were attached to the ceiling. In the center of the room stood a tall brass censer. Something smoldered in the center, emitting billows of bluish smoke.

As Smith reached for a handkerchief to cover his stinging nostrils, Chiun pulled a red silk pouch from his sleeve and sprinkled a powder into the censer. A brief flame flared up and the smoke intensified.

"Observe," Chiun said.

He then walked to a wall and with arms outstretched attempted to pass through a leaning mirror. His long fingernails tapped the reflective surface. He pushed. The pane shattered, shards falling at Chiun's sandaled feet.

"You see?" Chiun said in an exasperated voice. "It does not work. Could you tell me what is wrong, the mirror or the smoke?"

"Excuse me?" Smith said as Remo hid a widening grin behind his hand.

"Is this the correct kind of mirror?" Chiun went on.

"Or is it that the smoke is not properly colored? I am inclined to think that the smoke is not blue enough, but Remo refuses to advise me."

Remo caught Smith's helpless sidelong glance.

"Blue smoke and mirrors," Remo whispered. "Chiun overheard Robin suggest it as a possible explanation. He's trying to crack the method."

"Uh, excuse me, Master of Sinanju," Smith ventured. "But the phrase 'blue smoke and mirrors' is just an expression. It's meaningless."

"That is what Remo told me, but I heard two different persons profess that the thief used blue smoke and mirrors to accomplish his nefarious deeds. I saw no evidence of this myself, but whites are so devious" —Chiun looked at Remo with special pointedness— "that I cannot be certain."

"I assure you, Master of Sinanju," Smith said, backing away from the smoke, his eyes tearing, "that the device used was electronic."

"Ah, electronic," Chiun murmured. "I understand now. But tell me, which was electronic—the smoke or the mirrors?"

And Remo burst out into such laughter that Smith never got a chance to answer. Chiun flew out of the room, slamming the door behind him so hard that the sound of breaking glass was a crescendo as he unleashed a torrent of invective in both Korean and English. Smith couldn't follow the Korean portion— and the English was delivered at such speed that he had trouble catching all of that too—but he was certain that Chiun called Remo "a pale piece of pig's ear" at least six times.

When Chiun finally subsided, he joined Remo and Smith at the kitchen table. His face was stormy and Remo had to hold up Chiun's end of the conversation as well as his own.

"This much we know," Smith was saying. "This agent worked out of the Soviet embassy in Washington, D.C. I have been tapping CIA intercepts of telephone and telex traffic between the embassy and Moscow. Much of it is in open code—mundane words used to substitute for critical terms—but I believe I have the general idea. It seems that the chargé d'affaires there is about to return to Moscow with unspecified stolen U.S. technology."

"But we recovered the stuff the guy lifted in North Dakota," Remo insisted.

"Yes, but that apparently represents only the most recent looting. I have been running checks on other military installations for phenomena such as occurred at LCF-Fox. Missing food and personal items. Things of that sort.'

"Yeah?"

Smith sighed. "Either U.S. military personnel are all stealing one another blind, or this pattern of activity has been going on for a long time."

"How long?"

"Two or three years."

"Years!" Remo exploded. "He's been ripping us off for years and nobody's even noticed?"

"I am afraid so. You must understand that we inventory so many parts with redundant backups and all, that missing components are often dismissed as bookkeeping errors. It's easier to call it that than to disrupt the status quo with a full-fledged investigation."

"Well, hip-hip-hooray for the U.S. serviceman, protector of his precious behind."

"But personal thefts are reported," Smith went on. "I have accumulated a list of missing blue jeans, personal computers, VCR's, and Walkmen."

"I think it's Walkmans," Remo said sourly.

"Whatever. These are exactly the kinds of items that are in demand on the Russian black market."

"Now, why would a Soviet agent risk his mission to lift stuff like that on the side?" Remo wondered. "When we caught up with him he was carrying steaks. That was all. Just steaks."

"Because he is stupid, like all Russians," Chiun interjected suddenly.

"It's because he's a kleptomaniac," Smith added.

"Kleptomaniac?" Remo asked. Chiun leaned closer, interest on his wise face.

"I presented my findings, disguised, of course, to Folcroft's head psychiatrist," Smith explained. "It's his reasoned belief that we are dealing with a classic compulsive kleptomaniac."

"I understand a maniac," Chiun said, glancing at Remo. "I live with one. But what is a klepto? Is it like a poltergeist?"

"A kleptomaniac is a person who has a compulsive mania to steal," Smith explained. "He cannot help himself. He will steal anything that catches his fancy, regardless of its value or the risk involved."

"You know, Chiun," Remo put in pointedly, "like certain persons who lift all the toothpicks and mints at restaurant cash registers."

"They are there for the benefit of customers," Chiun snapped back. "And I do not take them *all*. I leave some."

"Three or four out of fifty toothpicks is not some. It's a token gesture to your conscience. And you don't even eat candy."

"I give the mints to children," Chiun replied huffily. "Would you deny an old man the simple pleasure of sharing with children?"

"You charge them a nickel a pop."

"Only the ones who look as if they can afford to pay. The ragamuffins get them without cost."

"Could you two please stop this?" Smith said testily. "Time is of the essence."

"Yes, of course. The mission. Please forgive Remo's carping, Emperor. I do not know where he gets these ugly habits from."

Remo rolled his eyes ceilingward. He drummed his fingers on the kitchen table impatiently.

"As I was saying," Smith continued, "the chargé d'affaires is about to fly to Moscow. He's leaving from Dulles on an Aeroflot flight. And he will be carrying a case identical to this one."

"Really?" Chiun said, examining the case. "How do you know this?"

"This is a standard diplomatic case, nicknamed 'Jaws' because of its capaciousness."

"That means it is large," Chiun said for Remo's benefit.

"Thanks," Remo said dryly. "I caught the drift all by myself."

"Lucky you."

Smith cleared his throat. "Airport security people do not X-ray or inspect these cases when embassy officials carry them. I am certain that the chargé d'affaires will be carrying sensitive military parts in his case."

"He will not live to enjoy his ill-gotten gains," Chiun promised vehemently.

"No, that's exactly what we do *not* want," Smith said hastily. "You must not harm him. The diplomatic repercussions could be grave."

"Then let me suggest a tiny blow," Chiun said in a conspiratorial tone. "Harmless as a fly's bite at first, but three weeks later the victim drops dead from kidney failure. This service was very much in demand during Roman times."

"Please," Smith pleaded. "This must not get back to us in *any* way."

"It will not," Chiun said firmly. "I assure you."

"No," Smith said just as firmly. "I want to switch cases. That's all. Do it so he doesn't suspect the exchange has taken place. Can you accomplish this?"

"We will be as the drifting smoke in our stealth," Chiun promised. "The drifting *blue* smoke."

Remo opened the case. "It's empty," he said. "Won't he notice the switch?"

"Fill it with junk," Smith suggested.

Remo shut the case. "I don't do junk collecting," he said. "It's not in my job description."

"Do not fret, Emperor Smith," Chiun said. "I have just the thing."

"You do?" Smith said.

"He does," Remo said. "Fourteen steamer trunks full."

"I see," Smith said as he rose from his chair. "Here is a photograph of your target. His name is Yuli Batenin."

"Rice paper?" Remo asked, looking at the face.

"Don't be ridiculous."

"Who, me?"

Smith paused at the open back door. "By the way, did you dispose of those files?"

"Of course," Remo lied, suddenly remembering the files tucked into his back pocket.

"Good. And I suggest you clear this house of smoke before someone calls the fire department."

"Fear not, Emperor," Chiun called loudly. "We will serve your needs with skill and daring, for we honor your wisdom and your graciousness."

His patrician face embarrassed, Smith hastily closed the door after him.

"Why do you always raise your voice when he's got the door open?" Remo asked. "You know how he is about security."

Chiun shrugged, pulling the case off the table. "Perhaps it will encourage him to visit less often." He disappeared into another room.

A few minutes later, the racket coming from the attic was too much for Remo to ignore and he went up the folding stairs.

He found the Master of Sinanju dumping the contents of one of his steamer trunks into the diplomatic

valise. Remo noticed that the items included video-
tapes and phonograph albums.

Remo plucked up one of the latter as Chiun began
stuffing posters in between the heavier objects as
packing.

"Barbra Streisand's Greatest Hits?" Remo asked,
pointing to the smiling face on the album cover.

"When one has a retentive mind, one need listen to
a song but once and it will stay in the heart forever,"
Chiun said distantly.

"That's not what I meant. I thought you still har-
bored a crush on her—although I'll admit it's been a
long time since you've mentioned it."

"She has spurned me for too long."

"The love letters still coming back unopened, eh?"

Chiun shrugged his frail shoulders. "It is not that so
much. I assume that selfish sycophants around her are
responsible for that. But I lost respect for Barbra after
she took up with that mere boy."

"And who might that be?" Remo asked, handing
the album to Chiun. The Master of Sinanju snapped it
in two without hesitating and stuffed it into the case.
A framed portrait of Streisand followed it in, its glass
front cracked.

"I do not recall his name. John Donson, or something. He is the one on that absurd flamingo show.
Florida Lice, I think it is called."

"Florida . . .? Oh, that. Yeah. I can see how you'd
be upset, getting shut out by a twerp like that. I mean,
the guy must be . . . what, forty, fifty years younger
than you?"

"She could have had perfection," Chiun growled.
"Instead she settled for one who shows so little respect
for himself that he wears no socks and shaves only
once a week."

"I got news for you, Little Father. *Miami Vice* is off
the air, and I think Barbra Streisand dumped him long
ago."

"It is? She did?" Chiun looked up, his facial hair quivering with hope.

"Of course, that's just a rumor," Remo admitted. "It may not be true."

Chiun hesitated. Then he shredded the unauthorized Barbra Streisand life story—both the hardcover and paperback editions—into confetti and used them for packing as well.

"It no longer matters," the Master of Sinanju said resignedly. "That she kissed such a one as that is enough of an insult to my feelings."

"She actually kissed him, huh?"

"I know it is shocking, but I have it on excellent authority. Now I can never forgive, nor will I forget this humiliation."

Chiun slammed the case closed. Then, hands tucked into his sleeves, he marched, chin lifted high and only slightly quivering, to the ladder steps. He floated down them with stolid dignity. Only Remo recognized the square set of his thin shoulders as indicating a breaking heart.

"What about this case?" Remo called after him. "You gonna just leave it here?"

"No," Chiun returned dully. "You may carry it."

"Why not?" Remo muttered. hefting the case. "I've been carrying your spear for years." It was surprisingly heavy. He hoped it weighed as much as a case full of stolen military equipment.

Outside, Remo placed the case in the trunk of his blue Buick. It felt strange to think of a car as his. He used to rent cars exclusively for security reasons, often leaving them in remote locations so that the rental bills would go through the roof. But now that he had a permanent home, Remo figured security wouldn't suffer from owning a permanent car too—although he missed Smith's howls of protest when the rental bills came in.

Chiun was already in the passenger seat when Remo

got behind the wheel. The Master of Sinanju stared ahead woodenly.

"When we get back," he said in a low, bitter voice, "remind me to speak to Smith about John Donson."

Remo started the engine. "What about him?"

"I have heard rumors that he has a criminal past."

"I think you're confusing the TV role with the actor."

"We shall see. But perhaps Smith's computer things will turn up something, and I can persuade him to allow me to punish Donson for his vicious infractions committed against the glorious American Constitution. In God We Trust."

Remo grunted. "I'm glad you're taking this so well."

"Masters of Sinanju learn how to bear up under disappointment," Chiun sniffed, rearranging his kimono skirts primly. "Besides, there is always Cheeta Ching, the beautiful Korean anchorperson."

"Isn't she married now?"

Chiun's voice dropped to a conspiratorial whisper. "I have written to her about her husband. He has been laying hands on other women, the pervert."

"How do you know that?" Remo asked as he backed out of the driveway.

"He is a gynecologist," Chiun hissed. "He admits this."

"No!" Remo said in a mock-serious voice.

Chiun nodded seriously. "They are worse than kleptomaniacs. Believe me, Remo. Cheeta will be eternally grateful for the information I have provided her."

"If it works out, can I be your best man?"

"No. When a Master of Sinanju marries, there is only one best man in attendance. And that is the bridegroom."

"Oh," Remo said in a small voice.

Chiun reached out to touch Remo on the arm.

"Oh, do not fret, my son. I have not forgotten you. You may be second-best man at my wedding. Or third. Possibly fourth. But no lower than fourth. Unless, of course, you disgrace me in some horrible way. Then I might demote you to fifth-best-man position. But that is the absolutely lowest, unless—"

"I get the picture," Remo snapped, pressing the accelerator harder. He promised himself that he would grab the window seat on the flight down, and to hell with Chiun's protests about having to have a clear view of the wings in case they started to fall off.

12

Major Yuli Batenin hummed "Moscow Nights" contentedly. He looked forward to going home after so long.

Most would consider the Washington-embassy post the plum assignment in the Soviet diplomatic corps. Or in the KGB, for that matter, for Yuli Batenin was first and foremost KGB station chief in Washington. He was attached to the Soviet embassy as chargé d'affaires.

But as the white embassy compound receded in the narrow rear window of the ambassador's Lincoln Continental, Yuli Batenin did not look back. Washington was fine. America was fascinating, but this particular assignment had gone on too long. When he reached Moscow and handed over the latest plunder from U.S. installations, Batenin would request a new posting. Three years was enough.

Of course his KGB superiors would ask him why.

And Major Batenin would tell them. He was certain they would understand.

It was not America, he would say in the *dusha-dushe*—heart-to-heart—talk he envisioned. It was not the embassy. It was not even the devious Captain Rair Brashnikov. Exactly. Batenin could handle the diminutive thief. True, it was annoying to have to search Brashnikov's room when he was away in order to recover personal effects belonging to the embassy staff, but it was a small price to pay for the great technological gains that were being realized through Operation Nimble Spirit. Batenin understood that. Certain sacrifices were necessary.

It was not that he would have to report that after nearly three years of unsuspected operations, their agent had been seen. He had not been captured. He had not been identified. No one even knew he was a Russian, so far as Batenin knew. True, for the first time, stolen U.S. property had not been delivered to the embassy on schedule. No doubt those items were now in the hands of puzzled American CIA agents.

That was acceptable. Major Batenin felt certain that one blemish in what was otherwise the most flawless long-term KGB operation ever conducted in the western hemisphere would be overlooked.

But, Batenin intended to say, there were some things that were too much to bear.

It was simply, Yuli Batenin considered as he watched the immaculate shrubbery of Washington streak by the tinted car window, the Jaws travel case handcuffed to his left wrist, that things had gotten just too strange.

His superiors would naturally have an answer to that. Of course it is strange, they might say. You have charge of an agent who walks through walls and cannot be touched by human hands.

Batenin would reply that he had gotten used to that. It had become almost normal.

What was not normal was nearly succumbing to a heart attack from simply answering the telephone. That was not normal. It was too much. He would not want to go through it again. In fact, he had developed nightmares as a result. Now when the phone rang, Major Yuli Batenin would jump like a startled cat.

For Major Batenin, generally regarded as one of the KGB's best station chiefs, had developed a severe telephone phobia.

It had happened two days ago, and Yuli still shivered at the memory.

A phone call had come in through the embassy switchboard. Major Batenin was in his office at the time, inventorying the latest military acquisitions, and eagerly anticipating the next group, which were being collected at a North Dakota missile grid. He remembered reaching for the intercom to ask who was calling. It was a simple thing, something he had done many times before.

"Ivan Grozny," he was told.

It was Brashnikov's alias. Batenin recalled saying, "I will take it," and switching off the intercom. He pushed the line-four button on his telephone—even the number four haunted him now—and picked up the receiver.

A simple act, this picking up of a telephone receiver. Major Batenin had picked up possibly a hundred thousand telephone receivers in his long career. He had no reason to suspect that this was anything other than a routine contact call.

He had placed the receiver to his ear. The sound of static was very loud. It was odd. Usually U.S. telephone lines were quite clear. This one crackled and whooshed. Mostly it whooshed.

"Hello?" he had asked.

The whooshing grew. Soon it was a roar.

"Hello?" Batenin had repeated. He heard voices. A mixture of voices in the receiver. None of them belonged to Rair Brashnikov. "Hello, Brashnikov? Are you there?" Batenin blurted out, annoyed. What foolish games was that thief up to now?

Only growing static answered him.

"Brashnikov! Speak! Answer me."

It was only because the roar of static grew unendurable that Yuli Batenin knew something was terribly wrong. He yanked the receiver from his ear. It was a fortunate thing that he did so, for who knew what might have happened had he not?

It all happened in an instant of time, but it would remain seared in Yuli Batenin's memory forever.

He had just jerked the receiver away when there came a sharp spitting sound from the earpiece, followed by a flash of supernatural brightness.

"Chort vozmi!" Yuli swore, inadvertently dropping the phone. He clutched at his eyes. The light had blinded him. He stumbled against his chair, cracking one knee.

"Govno!" he howled, falling to the rug. Taking his hairy hand from his eyes, he blinked furiously. He could not see the room. All was white.

"Help me," he cried helplessly. "I am blinded! Help me!"

Yuli Batenin heard the door open and his secretary call his name. Then, inexplicably, she screamed. The door slammed shut. He could hear her high heels clop away clumsily.

"Where are you going?" he cried. "I need help. I cannot see. Help me. Anyone. I am blind," Major Batenin cried. His face settled to the rug, which smelled of old shampoo, and he began sobbing.

The next several minutes were a maelstrom of white noise. He heard voices, cries. And then strong hands took him by the arms and lifted him to his feet.

By this time, the white brightness that his eyes perceived when the lids were closed had faded to a shimmery gray. He feared that it would go black next.

"Batenin," the Soviet ambassador was shouting. "How do we get him down? Tell us!"

"Blind. I am blind," Yuli repeated dazedly. "Help me. I want to go home. Take me back to Moscow."

"Open your eyes," he was told sternly.

"Blind!" Batenin sobbed.

"Open them!" Then he felt a hard smack against his cheek. Startled, his eyes flew open.

"Blind!" he repeated. But when he blinked, he could see again. "See! I can see. I am not blind!" he shouted happily.

"Get hold of yourself, Major. We need your knowledge. He is your man. How do we get him down?"

"Who? How?" Batenin asked shakily as he steadied himself against his desk.

He became aware of others in the room. They were standing in one corner of his office, broomsticks and desk blotters in their hands. They were swatting the air, as if at a pesky fly.

But it was not a fly that excited the embassy staff, Yuli saw to his horror.

For floating silently above the ducking and weaving heads of the embassy staff was a faintly luminous apparition.

"Brashnikov!" Batenin cried hoarsely.

"We cannot make contact with him, Batenin," the ambassador bit out. "And he is floating toward the wall. What can we do?"

Yuli Batenin pushed the ambassador aside as he stepped under the floating figure, his left knee wobbly with pain.

"Give me that," he ordered his secretary, relieving her of a broomstick.

He flipped the broomstick around until he had the straw end up in the air. He poked it at Brashnikov's eerily silent form.

The straw disappeared into Brashnikov's chest, as if swallowed by a cloud of milk.

"Is it ghost?" his secretary asked, horror in her voice.

Batenin withdrew the broom. Brashnikov's blisterlike face was distended like a clam's stomach. It neither contracted nor expanded. Brashnikov was not breathing. His arms and legs were splayed like a dead swimmer's. He floated on his stomach, just under the ceiling.

As Batenin watched, Brashnikov seemed to be drifting toward one wall. It was an outer wall.

"We must stop him!" Batenin suddenly cried. "If he floats away, it will be as if we raised flag over official Washington proclaiming Soviet responsibility for their technological losses."

"How?" the ambassador demanded. "We have tried everything."

"Have you tried blowing at him?"

"What?"

"He is floating like balloon. Let us all get under him and blow mightily."

It took a moment for the thought to register, but finally the ambassador shrugged as if to say: What have we to lose?

The embassy staff stooped down under Brashnikov's silent, hovering body, their backs to the outer wall.

"Everyone," Batenin ordered, "take deep breath. Ready? Now . . . exhale!"

They all blew hot streams of air at the body. But there was no perceptible reaction.

"Again!" Batenin called.

They tried again. They huffed and they puffed, until their faces grew purple and some of them became dizzy from oxygen deprivation.

They ended up sprawled on the rug, out of breath. Batenin looked up dazedly. If anything, Brashnikov had inched closer to the outer wall. In another few minutes his left hand would drift into the wall itself.

"He is dead?" the ambassador wheezed.

"*Da,*" Batenin gasped. "He breathes not."

"Then there is nothing we can do to stop him?"

"*Nyet.* Perhaps he will float out to sea."

"Moscow will not be happy that we have lost the suit."

Yuli Batenin looked up helplessly. If only there was a way . . .

And then he saw something that, had he not been

so soul-shocked by the events of the last half-hour, he would have noticed long before this.

"Oh, God, no," Yuli breathed.

"What . . . what is wrong?"

"His belt light," Yuli said, pointing shakily. "It is red."

"*Da*," the ambassador said. "So?"

"It means that he is on emergency power supply." Batenin looked at his watch. "There is less than a half-hour until the suit shuts itself off."

The ambassador's dour face brightened.

"That is good, *da*?"

"That is bad, *nyet*," Yuli said, finding his feet. He didn't take his eyes off Brashnikov's floating form. "If the suit shuts itself off now, he will drop to rug and all will be well. But if he floats into wall, and suit shuts off then, there is no accounting for what could happen."

"What are the possibilities?" the ambassador asked. He had not been briefed on the vibration suit's operational details.

"It is possible Brashnikov's body will become permanently stuck in wall. In which case we need only replace wall."

"A minor inconvenience under circumstance."

"The other possibility is nuclear."

"Nuclear!" This came from almost everyone in the room in a single breath.

"If atoms mix," Batenin told them, "they may shatter. The result will be atomic explosion."

The ambassador jumped to his feet. "Quickly. We must evacuate embassy."

"No," Yuli said dully, still looking at the immobile blister face only inches above him. "How far could we get in less than one-half hour? Not enough to clear Washington outskirts. And if there is splitting of atoms, it will be many, many atoms splitting. Too many to count." He shook his head. "No, we are better off here, where our end will be swift and painless. For if suit goes dead at wrong time, all of Washington will be obliterated. Perhaps much of eastern seaboard as well."

The embassy staff all looked at one another in white-faced terror. And, as if telepathically inspired, they leapt to their feet and began blowing at the inexorably moving figure with all their combined lung power.

Even Yuli Batenin joined in, although he knew it was futile. But what else was there left for them to do—lie down and die?

It happened just before the tips of Rair Brashnikov's still fingers brushed the wallpaper. Without warning, the blister face constricted. Then it ballooned out. Another contraction. And a rhythm was established.

"He breathes!" Yuli shouted. "Brashnikov! Do you hear me? Turn off suit. Turn off vibration suit!"

Then the fingertips of Brashnikov's left hand disappeared into the wall.

"Oh, God," someone said hoarsely. Batenin's secretary ran from the room screaming.

"Rair . . ." Batenin was sobbing now. "The suit! Turn it off. Use your left hand. Please!"

The face membrane respirated. But Rair Brashnikov still floated inertly, his limbs splayed. Then the red light blinked. Batenin's eyes widened in terror. He never saw the vanished fingers of Rair Brashnikov withdraw from the wall as he stiffly attempted to reach his belt rheostat. Batenin's eyes were fixed on that red light whose extinguishing meant their lives.

Then the whole world seemed to fall on Yuli Batenin.

When he woke up in the embassy infirmary later, he was screaming.

"Nyet! Nyet! Nyet!"

The infirmary nurse attempted to calm him.

"Be a man, Comrade Major," the nurse admonished. She was a hulking blond who knew nothing of what had transpired in the office two floors above.

"I live," Yuli breathed. It was more of a prayer than a question.

"*Da*. Comrade Brashnikov will survive too. He had a nasty fall. It was fortunate that you were there to throw yourself under him to break it, otherwise he would have been severely injured."

Yuli Batenin turned his head. In the next bed, Rair Brashnikov lay with a white sheet pulled up to his sharp chin. His ferretlike profile was peaceful. He snored contentedly.

Major Batenin's nervous reaction to the sight of Brashnikov was so violent that he had to be sedated.

A calmer Batenin himself debriefed Brashnikov the next morning. Brashnikov's story was disjointed and Batenin did not believe much of it. He was certain that Brashnikov was holding something back. He did not know what. Brashnikov had spent much more time in North Dakota than had been necessary. What had he been doing there? Brashnikov insisted that penetrating underground launch facilities had been very difficult.

Later, Batenin conferred with the technician on staff who maintained the suit.

"He claims he was in North Dakota, making call to this embassy when he was surprised in hotel room," Batenin explained. "He turned on suit. He remembers rushing through dark tunnel. He thought himself dead. The next he knew he crashed to floor of my office. Tell me, how can this be?"

The technician considered.

"This tunnel," he asked, "was it a long straight tunnel?"

"No. He said it twisted and turned."

"Hmmmm. We do not fully understand the suit's many properties," the technician said slowly. "But as you know, when it is on, the atoms of the body are in an unstable state, as are the component protons, neutrons, and electrons."

"Yes, of course. I know all that."

"Electricity is composed of electrons. It is possible—

theoretically possible—that teleportation might have been achieved."

"I do not know that word," Batenin had admitted.

"A theoretical fantasy," the technician supplied. "One that postulates that if it were possible to disassemble a person or an object on the molecular level, it should also be possible to transmit those elements, as electricity is transported through wire or cable, to another place, there to be reconstituted into its original form."

"I fail to—"

"Imagine a fax machine," the technician said. "One which, instead of producing a duplicate copy of a document at another site, transmits the original document, which ceases to exist at the point of origin."

"Are you saying that Brashnikov *faxed* himself through telephone?"

"I do not think it was intentional. How could he know? As he said, he was talking into an open-line receiver. He turned on the suit. Somehow his free-floating electrons were conducted into the receiver, taking his other atomic particles with them, and transmitted out the other end."

Batenin shuddered at the memory of the incredible white light that had blinded him.

"And the tunnel he described?" Batenin prompted.

"Wire or fiberoptic cables," the technician assured him. "The Americans use both for voice transmission."

"This accident. Might it be duplicated?"

"If it worked once, it should work again. But I would not advise a repetition of the experience. It obviously had a traumatic effect on the agent. He was not breathing when he emerged from the receiver."

"Perhaps he will become used to the experience," Batenin said thoughtfully. "Thank you for your analysis."

Yuli Batenin had already made his decision when he visited Brashnikov in the infirmary.

The Russian was already sitting up, eating ice cream.

He had developed a suspect addiction to American foods.

"I am returning to Moscow, captain," Yuli told him stiffly after explaining the technician's theory to the interested thief.

"I will be here when you get back," Rair said, spooning out the nuts in the bowl of pistachio ice cream. He liked pistachio, but hated the nuts.

"I may not be coming back," Yuli told him. "I am going to ask for a new assignment. While I am in Moscow, see that you behave yourself until my replacement arrives. Then you will proceed with the operation."

Surprised, Rair Brashnikov had put down the bowl of ice cream.

"I am sorry to see you go," Brashnikov said, his black eyes shining like a fawn's. "You have been a good man to work with. And you saved me from bad fall, for which I am grateful."

Touched in spite of himself, Yuli Batenin nodded. "*Da*, I will miss you too, Brashnikov."

And when Rair reached out his arms to give him a farewell bear hug, Yuli returned the gesture, even though he had never liked the tiny thief.

Yuli had to struggle to extricate himself from the sentimental gesture.

With a stiff "Farewell, Tovarich Captain," Major Yuli Batenin exited the room, quickly picked up the diplomatic case, and entered the waiting limousine.

And now, as the limousine pulled up at his terminal at Dulles International Airport, Batenin was pleased and relieved that he would no longer have responsibility for such a high-risk operation as this.

With the big case still handcuffed to his wrist, Yuli Batenin strolled to the airport lounge. He ordered a C-breeze, and stared at his watch, while awaiting his departure time. He did not want to be seen in the waiting room, the case so obvious on his wrist. There were many thieves in America who would be attracted to the case for that very reason. Yuli hated thieves of all kinds.

When the boarding call finally came, Batenin drained the last of his drink and walked casually to the X-ray station. There was an armed guard in uniform standing by the metal-detector frame. Another man was operating the X-ray machine. Yuli barely noticed him. It would be the guard he would have to deal with. This shouldn't take more than a few moments.

Ignoring the metal detector, Batenin walked up to the guard and fixed him with a bold stare.

"I am Batenin, chargé d'affaires with the Soviet embassy," he said firmly, reaching for his wallet. He froze.

"I . . ." Yuli swallowed. "One moment, please," he said sheepishly, patting his inside coat pocket. It was empty. He tried the outer pockets. They too were empty. In vain, the perspiration streaming from his brow, he tried his pants pockets, although he knew that he never carried his wallet containing diplomatic identification there. America was full of pickpockets.

"I am afraid . . . that is, I seem to have left billfold in car," Yuli said in a sick voice as the loudspeaker announced the final boarding call for Aeroflot Flight 182.

"Do you have your ticket, sir?" the guard asked politely.

"Yes, yes. It is here," Yuli said in relief, plucking it from his shirt pocket. "But diplomatic identification is missing."

"There are a lot of thieves at this airport."

"Thieves?" Yuli said blankly. Then his facial expression changed to one of anger. He was thinking of a farewell bear hug from a man whom he despised. "Brashnikov," he hissed.

"Beg pardon?" the guard said.

"It is nothing," Batenin said quickly. "Please. I beg you. I must make flight."

"Certainly. But without ID, I'll have to ask you to go through the metal detector. And your valise will have to be X-rayed."

Yuli Batenin looked over to the X-ray machine. The operator was looking at him with an innocent expression. He had the deadest eyes Yuli had ever seen. Like nail holes.

"I'm afraid I must insist. For I have diplomatic immunity."

"I don't doubt that," the guard said firmly. "But without documentation, you'll have to go through the same security procedures as everyone else. It's for your own safety, sir."

"But I cannot," Yuli sputtered. "For key to handcuffs in missing wallet. You cannot expect me to go through X-ray device with case. I would not fit."

Yuli gave the guard a helpless smile. In truth, the key was nestled in his left shoe.

The guard looked to the dead-eyed X-ray operator.

"How do we handle this?" he asked.

"No problem," the other man said helpfully. "We can X-ray the case without it going all the way through the belt."

"But . . . but . . ." Batenin sputtered.

"If it's a problem, you can miss your flight," the guard said. "We can't *make* you go through security, but you can't board your plane unless you do. Your choice, sir."

The thought of having to return to the embassy and to that thief Brashnikov, whose scrawny neck he would like to strangle, flicked through Major Batenin's panicky mind. He decided to take the chance. Anything was better than another day on this operation.

"Very well," Batenin said stiffly. "I give consent."

"Fine. Now, since you can't go through the metal

detector, I'll have to pat you down. Just take a moment."

Clutching the case with both hands, Yuli Batenin allowed himself to endure the indignity of being frisked. When that ordeal was over, he was escorted to the X-ray device.

"Just put it down on the belt," the operator told him cheerfully. He shut down the conveyor belt.

He was a very happy menial, Yuli noticed. Usually airport security people were as grave of face as a statue of Stalin, but this one seemed quite eager to be of help. Perhaps this would not be so bad. For he doubted that the X-ray would show anything that an untrained person would consider suspicious.

Yuli complied. The operator jabbed a button several times to make the conveyor belt inch forward. The case disappeared into the innards of the X-ray machine, Yuli's right hand following it in right up to the elbow.

"Will this hurt?" Yuli asked awkwardly. He had to lean on the machine to keep his balance. This was very difficult.

"Just hold that pose," the operator told him. Then he pressed a button. He pressed it again.

"What is wrong?" Yuli demanded nervously.

"Minor glitch. Be just another second. Don't worry."

"I do not want my hand to be X-rayed to what you Americans call a crisp."

"Not a chance," the operator assured him. He tapped the machine again. It seemed to tap back. And then the operator smiled.

"Okay," he said brightly, "you can pull it out now."

Batenin pulled the familiar case out again. He looked at his hand fearfully, but appeared not to be discolored from overexposure.

Nodding to the guard, the X-ray operator said, "He checks out. Let him through."

Major Batenin inclined his head to the two Americans as diplomatically as he could and hurried to the gate, muttering curses on the head of Rair Brashnikov under his breath.

The aircraft doors were locked after Yuli boarded. The moment he sat down, he felt the cold perspiration soaking his suit. But he breathed a slow sigh of relief.

But just to be certain, he kicked off one shoe and extracted the key as the wide-bodied Ilyushin-96 backed away from the gate. He put the key in the lock and twisted. The key would not turn. He forced it. It broke in the lock.

"What?" he muttered. Then he noticed that the bracelet attached to the case's handle was warped. He looked closer. It was fused at the locking point. It had not been that way during the drive. Could the multiple X-rays have fused the metal? he wondered anxiously.

And what about the contents?

Yuli Batenin pulled another key from his right shoe. It would not open the case. Not at all.

Fiercely, fearing the worst, he tore at the case with fingers like hooks. He broke his nails in the process, but by sheer might he ripped away one corner of the case.

Bits of torn paper fluttered out. There had been no paper in Batenin's case. Anxiously he dug his fingers in. They came away red. He had cut them on something. Glass.

"There was no glass in this case," he howled aloud.

Digging further, he found a slick sheet of paper. It looked like a page from a book or magazine. There was a color photograph printed on it. A woman's face. Yuli Batenin thought the face was familiar. It took him until the Aeroflot flight had rolled into position for takeoff before he recognized the face of the famous American singer and actress Barbra Streisand.

"Let me off plane!" Batenin screamed. "I must get off!"

*   *   *

Back at the X-ray station, the operator pointed out to the guard that foot traffic had finally quieted down.

"Wanna get us both a cup of coffee?" he suggested.

"Sure. Take it black?"

"Yeah, black is fine," said Remo, to whom a cup of coffee was the equivalent to a dose of strychnine.

After the guard had disappeared around the corner, Remo rapped on the X-ray device and whispered, "It's okay, Chiun. You can come out now."

The Master of Sinanju slithered out of the compartment with a distasteful expression on his parchment face. He hauled a big boxy case with him.

"Next time, I will handle the buttons and you will hide inside," he hissed.

"Let's hope there isn't a next time," Remo said, taking the case. "And I apologize for the long wait. How was I to know he'd wait until the very last minute to board?"

"At least we did not have to resort to further subterfuge to make him relinquish his case."

"Yeah," Remo said as they walked away. "Funny how that worked out. I must've shown my FAA ID card to thirty or forty airline reps before they'd let me sub for the regular X-ray operator, and then had to coach the guard over and over to pretend the guy's diplomatic card had expired so we could get at the case. He was so nervous, I was positive he was going to blow it. And what happens? The Russian loses his ID. Must be my lucky day."

"Next time, I will handle the buttons," Chiun repeated as they sat down in a quiet corner of a waiting area.

"You know how you are with machines. Something could have gone wrong." Remo looked into the case. His face fell. "Uh-oh, I think something did."

"What?" Chiun asked quickly, leaning over to see.

"You did switch cases, didn't you?"

"Do you doubt my prowess?" Chiun asked huffily.

"No, but I think we've been rooked. Look."

Remo held up an assortment of squares, like graphite tiles. Except they were a flat unreflective black and seemingly nonmetallic.

"What are these?" Chiun asked.

"Got me," Remo said quietly. "They look like Dracula's bathroom tiles. One thing for sure, they're not missile components or anything of the kind."

"Then you have failed," Chiun said coldly.

"Me? You did the switch."

"But you pressed the buttons."

Remo sighed. "Let's grab the next flight home. Maybe Smith can make sense of things," he said, sending the tiles clattering back into the case.

They went in search of a flight back to New York.

"You were not tricked," Dr. Harold W. Smith told them firmly. Smith was sitting in his cracked leather chair at Folcroft Sanitarium. The big picture window behind him framed Long Island Sound. Smith soberly turned one of the black tiles over and over in his thin hands.

"No?" Remo asked, pleased.

"I told you so," Chiun squeaked. "You worry too much, Remo. Imagine, Emperor, Remo left the critical task of switching cases to me and he had the audacity to suggest that I could make a mistake."

"Thanks a lot, Chiun," Remo muttered.

"These are RAM tiles," Smith said bitterly.

"Ah, of course, I have seen their commercials on TV," Chiun said pleasantly. "They are a big company. Perhaps they will agree to sponsor us in gratitude for recovering their valuable property."

"I doubt that," Smith replied dryly. "RAM is not a brand name. It stands for Radar-Absorbing Material. These tiles are made of a top-secret carbon-epoxy composition, and constitute the skin of our new generation of Stealth aircraft. It is fortunate, Remo, that you intercepted these before they reached Moscow."

"Remo?" Chiun squeaked. "It was I who made the exchange. Brilliantly, I might add."

Smith cleared his throat. "Yes. Of course I meant both of you," he said.

"Remo just pressed unimportant buttons," Chiun said pointedly. "Anyone could have done that. A monkey could have performed Remo's task. I, on the other hand, performed the all-important exchange completely unsuspected by our adversary. Would you like to hear the story again, Emperor?"

"Er, no. Not just now," Smith said hastily. "I'm sorry. But let's stay on the subject. These particular tiles are from the Stealth bomber. There is only one place they could have come from and that is their point of manufacture, the Northrop Corporation facility in Palmdale, California, known as Plant Forty-two."

"These grow from plants?" Chiun asked, examining one tile.

"We have no leads on our thief," Smith said, ignoring him. "But these tiles tie in with the rash of Stealth crashes we've been having."

"How so, Smitty?" Remo asked with interest. Chiun pretended to examine his long curved nails. There was no sense in paying attention to whites when they rambled on in their unnecessary details. Let Remo explain the salient items later.

"What we know of the near-launch at Fox-4 tells us that this thief is capable of removing working parts from operational equipment. Suppose he extracted critical elements from hangared Stealth aircraft? If this went undetected, then the string of inexplicable Stealth failures is understandable."

Remo snapped his fingers. "I get it," he said. "They crashed because they were missing components."

"Exactly. And who would suspect that an unaccounted-for piece of Stealth wreckage had been extracted before the crash? At the same time, it would be impossible to steal sample tiles from a working aircraft because they are bonded to the frame." Smith paused. "He had to obtain them from the manufac-

turer. And if the Soviets are attempting to develop a
wing of Stealth aircraft of their own from our parts,
they cannot accept this setback. They must acquire
more tiles, otherwise the components they do have are
valueless."

"You think our *Krahseevah* will try for these again?"
Remo asked, hefting one of the tiles in his hand. It
was unusually light.

"The Soviets have no choice. They may not move
for weeks or even months, but unless a better lead
develops, you and Chiun will guard the Palmdale
facility."

"You haven't told us what we do to the *Krahseevah*
if we meet him again," Remo mentioned.

Smith's face fell.

"I have no answer for that, Remo," he said helplessly. "I only wish I did. But at the very minimum,
your mission is to keep any more RAM tiles from
falling into Soviet hands."

"We'll do what we can," Remo promised.

"Remo will do what he can," Chiun said acidly. "I
will do what you wish. As always."

"Don't mind him," Remo told Smith. "He's just in
a snotty mood because he didn't get a window seat on
the flight back. Probably not on the flight to California, either, the way he's acting."

Rair Brashnikov was feeling better. He was sitting
up in bed and ready to eat solid foods. The embassy
kitchen was preparing a thick London-broil steak for
him. He would have preferred porterhouse, and he
thought wistfully of the steaks he had had to leave
behind in North Dakota. He didn't mind the missile
parts that he could not bring with him. He was not
paid for each item stolen, receiving only his monthly
salary. He wondered what was wrong with Kremlin
thinking that they offered a man no incentive to excel
at the tasks given him to perform.

For three years now Rair had contented himself with stealing a little here and there for Mother Russia, and stealing a lot for himself. Every week he shipped big packages to his cousin Radomir in Soviet Georgia. And he knew that every week his cousin sold them on the black market for American dollars. Quite a pile of dollars would be awaiting Rair when he returned to Russia. If he ever did. After all, it was very nice in America. And it would be nicer now that Batenin was no longer around to bother him.

Footsteps sounded outside the dispensary door and Rair Brashnikov sat up straighter in anticipation of a London-broil steak and salty french fries on the side.

But these footsteps were heavy and menacing. Rair's thin dark brows puckered. There was an unmistakably familiar sound to them.

"Nyet," he muttered. "It could not be."

But when the door slammed open and Major Yuli Batenin stood framed in it, huge shoulders heaving, Rair Brashnikov frantically reached for his belt-buckle rheostat.

His hand encountered only the drawstring of his pajamas.

And then Batenin was on him like an avalanche. Brashnikov felt himself being hauled out of bed and slammed against the wall.

"Where is it?" Batenin demanded vehemently, the force of his words expelling hot saliva on Brashnikov's shrinking features.

"Tovarich, what is wrong?" Brashnikov asked innocently.

Major Batenin slapped him across the face once. Then again with the back of his hand. Rair's cheeks stung.

"Under mattress," Rair said fearfully, recognizing blazing, naked hatred in the other man's eyes.

Batenin dropped him, and Brashnikov collapsed on the floor.

He watched as Yuli Batenin rooted around under the mattress. In frustration he heaved the mattress off its springs with both arms. It was a heavy mattress. Brashnikov was impressed by the major's strength. Or possibly it was not mere strength, but sheer rage that empowered him so.

Brashnikov shrank into a corner of the room, awaiting the worst.

When Major Batenin straightened up, his wallet in hand, he turned to Brashnikov, his eyes fierce.

"If you ever steal from me again, I will wring your neck like a chicken's," he said in a too-low voice. "Do you understand, Brashnikov?"

"*Da, da,* Tovarich Major. I am sorry. It is merely irresistible urge that comes over me. I cannot help myself."

Batenin's red face was suddenly nose-to-nose with his own.

"I understand, Tovarich Brashnikov," Batenin said in a tone like grinding teeth.

"You do?"

"*Da.*" He sneered. "I am even now seized by compulsion. Only mine does not urge me to steal. Only to break your thieving neck. I will make deal with you. I will smother my compulsion if you control yours."

"Deal," Rair Brashnikov said, gulping. The major's alcoholic breath filled his nose with fumes.

"Now, Brashnikov," Batenin said, straightening up, "I would advise you to get well soon. By dawn at very latest. You have important task before you."

"I do?"

"You are going back to place where Stealth tiles are made. You will obtain more."

"I did not obtain enough?" Brashnikov asked in a puzzled voice.

"If I have to explain, I may lose control of myself," Batenin warned. "And neither of us wish that—do we?"

"*Nyet, nyet,*" Brashnikov said, shaking his head.

"Good. Because until more tiles are in my hands, I cannot return to Moscow. And as long as I am stuck in embassy, your safety is in doubt. Are we in agreement on this, Brashnikov?"

"I feel much better already," Brashnikov told him. He cracked a lopsided, ingratiating smile.

14

Plant Forty-two of Northrop's high-security Palmdale facility was a completely windowless corrugated-steel building painted the color of the surrounding desert sands. No one who toiled within its fortresslike walls ever saw daylight during the working day. This unusual construction was necessary because of the number of special-access, or "black-budget," defense projects that were hatched within its austere confines. Spies both industrial and international were everywhere. And in today's world of high-tech espionage, a window was an open invitation to everything from a parabolic microphone to orbiting reconnaissance satellites.

The problem with having no windows was that while it inhibited opportunities for spying or invasion, it also made it more difficult to detect approaching threats.

"No windows," Remo said. "Great." He and Chiun watched the building from behind their rented car. It was parked on a lonely highway some distance from the barbed-wire-ringed facility. "We can get really close to the building without being seen."

They were out in a scrub-desert area of California. Telephone poles quaked in the brittle heat. In the distance were the sullen San Gabriel Mountains.

"Not necessarily," the Master of Sinanju said. "We are better off stationing ourselves far from this ʋcalled plant. For it will not be our objective to prevent the *Krahseevah* from gaining entrance to this place, but to follow him after he leaves it."

"Isn't that risky?" Remo said. "What if he gets away with another batch of RAM tiles?"

Chiun shrugged as if it were an inconsequential matter.

"He will attempt to enter in this smokelike state," Chiun intoned. "We will not be able to stop him in that case. But if we allow him to leave unchallenged and, to his lights, unobserved, he will be less careful. Then we will follow him to his lair and catch him unawares, recovering any stolen artifacts."

"I like it," Remo said. "It's direct and simple."

"I tailored it for your mentality," Chiun told him. Before Remo could formulate a reply, the Master of Sinanju went on. "We will split up. I will position myself to the northeast, so that two walls are always in sight of my incomparable eyes. You, Remo, will take the southwest. Try to stay awake."

"Thanks a bunch," Remo said dryly. "You know we could be here for weeks."

"We will do what we have to do. That creature has angered me. I will take special delight in capturing and punishing it."

"Okay by me. Let's just hope something breaks soon. This isn't exactly my idea of the perfect place for an indefinite roost. I guess if you're taking northeast, and we happen to be parked southwest of the place, that means I get to wait in the car, huh?"

Chiun turned to Remo with his parchment features etched with disdain.

"Of course . . ." he began.

Remo grinned.

". . . not," Chiun finished. "You will drive me to the northeast point of vantage and I will wait in the automobile."

"And what am I supposed to do?" Remo growled. "Walk back?"

"You have something against walking, you who are young and smooth of skin, with unnumbered years stretching before you?"

"All right, all right," Remo said, getting behind the wheel. The Master of Sinanju settled into the passenger seat without a sound. The door closed like an infant's midnight exhalation.

Later, after Remo had parked the car in the shelter of a ridge, he picked his way through the triple ring of barbed wire and into the multibuilding facility. He secreted himself in an alley near a loading dock and crouched under the lip of a garbage dumpster. Fortunately, Remo thought, regulating his breathing so that the air came in too slowly to stir the scent receptors in his sensitive nose, this was an industrial area. Instead of smelling like dead fish, rotted cheese, and other rancid food smells, this particular dumpster reeked of hot plastic and acetone.

Remo had settled down to a long wait. An occasional security guard drifted by. Remo, in shadow, avoided them easily. The trick was not to catch their eye. Keeping still was a big part of it. Human peripheral vision picked up even the slightest movement, while a person looking straight on often missed the most obvious dangers because they did not act like threats.

Not watching an enemy was the other half of successful concealment. What the eyes missed, other senses often picked up. No one—not even Chiun—had ever satisfactorily explained human intuition to him, but Remo knew that even the worst-trained ordinary man could sometimes feel eyes on him. So he always looked away when the guards came by, confident that he would not be seen or sensed.

He was not.

Long after midnight—Remo, who never wore a watch, knew it was exactly 3:44 A.M. because the last time he had happened to notice a clock it had been 10:06 and his biological clock told him that that was exactly five hours and thirty-eight minutes ago—he suddenly felt the air on his bare forearms lift in warning.

It was not cold, and even if it was, Remo should have been able to will his tightening flesh to relax. It would not. That meant an electrical phenomenon. Maybe the *Krahseevah*.

Remo slipped around behind the dumpster, looking for any sign of the creature.

The hair on his forearms grew stiffer. And the short hairs at the back of his neck rose up too. It was the identical sensation he had felt during his first encounter with the thing. Robin Green had reported exactly the same thing.

Remo was on his feet, staring up at the darkened edges of the surrounding buildings, when the *Krahseevah* walked by him as casually as a Sunday stroller.

Except that the *Krahseevah* was glowing like a misty moon with legs.

Remo faded back with alacrity. The speed and silence of the creature's abrupt appearance had taken even him by surprise. The *Krahseevah* had emerged from the steel tank of the garbage dumpster like an alien stepping out of the fifth dimension.

Remo watched it walk stiffly to the side of a building. It stuck its head in tentatively, paused, and then slipped inside.

Remo glided to the building's edge.

He stared around the corner. Down at the far end, the *Krahseevah*'s glowing blister face emerged from the ridged steel like a forming bubble. The face hesitated, expanding and contracting regularly; then the *Krahseevah* stepped free of the wall. It cleared an open parking area with jerky strides. Then it crouched beside a tan Firebird. It melted into the car, causing the dim interior to glow faintly.

Remo hung back, seeing the thing's featureless face hovering over the dashboard. Ludicrously, its gold-veined boots stuck out below the chassis. The head swiveled slowly. It was obviously being very cautious.

Then the *Krahseevah* stepped from the car and, hugging walls and concrete loading docks, made its way to the windowless Plant Forty-two building.

Remo decided that he'd better get back to the garbage dumpster, where he would have a clear view of the building, but be least likely to attract notice. He did so.

Long minutes crawled by. Remo's eyes were trained on the building, but he fretted inwardly. Would the *Krahseevah* come out this way? He wished there was some way to warn Chiun. But he knew the Master of Sinanju was alert. But the problem would be that if the *Krahseevah* moved too fast, there wouldn't be time to get word to Chiun.

The *Krahseevah* appeared less than fifteen minutes later. Its glowing head poked out of Plant Forty-two's hangar doors—the same doors out of which the first Stealth bomber had rolled for media cameras. Evidently satisfied, the head withdrew and the hands came out, followed by the chest and the knees. The *Krahseevah* stood, one arm crooked, in the open. Then, clutching what Remo took to be an armful of RAM tiles, it backtracked its approach, going to the car, pausing, then working its way to the nearby building again.

Remo slipped around the back of the dumpster. The hairs on his arm began to rise again.

When they were at maximum elevation, Remo knew the *Krahseevah* was practically on top of him. He sneaked a peek around the corner.

The *Krahseevah* emerged from the other side of the dumpster and walked through a raised concrete walkway. Its legs disappeared below the thigh, which made

it look as if it were wading through solid concrete. It
vanished into a wall.

Remo went up the side of the wall like a spider. He
crouched down on the roof, unseen in his black T-shirt
and chinos.

The *Krahseevah* came out of the building on the
other side and picked its way from object to object,
like an octopus through coral. Whenever it found something to hide in—a wall or a car—it did. Once it
scrunched down to conceal itself in a humming air-
conditioning unit set in concrete.

Remo followed it with his eyes as far as he could.
Then he floated to the ground and trailed it through
the maze of barbed wire. The *Krahseevah* seemed to
be heading north, which Remo hoped might mean
he'd have a chance to tip off Chiun.

As the industrial park fell behind, Remo spotted the
Krahseevah loping through open desert, toward the
highway. Remo hung back to see if he could spot the
Master of Sinanju.

Their rented car was about a mile down the road,
which forked so that the car sat on the low road, in the
shadow of a ridge. The high road climbed the ridge.

It was too far for Remo to attract Chiun's attention. Frowning, he returned to trailing the *Krahseevah*.
The creature was moving from telephone pole to telephone pole, repeating its old tricks, Remo saw.

Then it stopped. As Remo watched, its lambent
glow faded.

It had turned off the suit.

Remo moved. He knew this would be his one chance.
He flashed through the desert, his toes making only
tiny wedge-shaped marks in the sand, he was running
so fast.

Then the low growl of an ignition sounded. A car!
The *Krahseevah* had a car waiting.

The car was a big one. A black Cadillac. Its taillights flared; then it backed out of the shadows, stopped, and purred down the highway.

It was heading for the fork in the road.

"Damn!" Remo said, shifting direction. If it took the low road, it would pass Chiun. But if it took the high road, the Master of Sinanju might assume it was only a passing car.

Remo decided to take the ridge. He sprinted harder. Let Chiun be pissed for missing out. There was no way to avoid it.

Remo cut across the highway and hit the bottom of the ridge at full speed. Without pausing, he transferred his running motion into a four-limbed climb. He went up the rocks like a beetle fleeing a grass fire. Momentum took him halfway up before he needed to exert any effort. His hands and feet found plenty of handholds.

Remo levered himself up to the road just in time to spot the Cadillac's taillights whisk by like retreating eyes. The car was accelerating rapidly. Remo took off after it. They hit the downhill slope, so gravity helped carry him along. Not that he needed gravity's help. Remo's toes dug into the heat-softened blacktop like climbing spikes. Dig, pause, and push. Left and right. Right and left. Loosened granules of tar kicked up behind him. And soon he was running as fast as the speeding Cadillac, which had to run with its brake drums touching the wheel rims to negotiate the steep slope. Remo caught up with the car. Then he was running with the Cadillac, as if the car were merely coasting.

Rair Brashnikov was pleased with himself. He had successfully penetrated the high-security Northrop facility once again. It was easier this second time, for he had already explored the best approaches the first time. The RAM tiles were in the same storage area. It was a simple matter to shut down the suit, scoop up an armful, and turn the belt rheostat so that his glowing body was once more impervious to bullets and obstacles.

As he had last time, Brashnikov had left a parked car nearby. It was too far to walk to the nearest town, and although there was an added risk in removing his helmet and battery pack after shutting down the vibration suit in order to get behind the wheel and drive off, the risk was more than offset by the convenience.

Now, hurtling through the still California desert night, Rair Brashnikov watched the road ahead as it flattened out and became a twisting blacksnake toward freedom. He only hoped that these tiles would be enough to satisfy Major Batenin and that the chargé d'affaires would shortly return to Moscow. Brashnikov feared that he had pushed the KGB major too far the last time. The man now had blood in his eyes whenever he saw Brashnikov, although the embassy buzzed with the rumor that Batenin would start at even the slightest sound. Especially ringing telephones.

Rair Brashnikov heard the sound before he realized he was being followed. There were no lights out here in the deserted highway, so the road ahead was a constantly changing splash of headlight glare. Behind him all was blackness and speeding telephone poles.

The sound seemed far away at first. It sounded like the distant wail of a siren. He wondered if it was an alarm being sounded back at Plant Forty-two. But the sound seemed to be drawing closer, as if it were a pursuing police car. But his rearview mirror showed only a wall of night. No pursuing vehicles at all.

Then Brashnikov happened to notice the man running alongside the car. He was all in black, so it was hard to make him out in the dim backglow of his headlights. But it was definitely a man.

Brashnikov looked down at his speedometer. It registered sixty-one miles an hour. That could not be, he thought to himself. There was a man keeping pace with his car. If the car was going sixty-one miles an hour, then it stood to reason that the man had to be going sixty-one miles an hour too. Maybe he was on skates.

Brashnikov swerved away from the man and took a look. No, the man was not on skates. He was running.

Then the man drifted—that was what it looked like, despite his speed—up to the driver's window. He knocked. Brashnikov looked up. He could not make out the runner's face. The man's mouth was wide open, yet he didn't seem to pant from exertion, as a man should who was running sixty-one miles an hour. The man's knuckles rapped on the driver's window again.

Brashnikov cracked the window open and the siren sound was suddenly very loud. Holding the wheel steady, he twisted around, but saw no pursuing car. Then Brashnikov realized that the sound was much closer. Almost at his elbow. Almost . . .

With a start he realized that it was coming from the running man. Crazily, insanely, he was making the noise with his mouth, like a child pretending to be a fire truck.

This was proved beyond any doubt when the man said, "Pull over." The siren sound stopped when he gave the order. Then it resumed again, this time louder.

"What is this?" Brashnikov demanded, reaching under the seat cushions carefully, one hand still on the wheel.

"I said, 'Pull over,' " the man repeated. "You're supposed to pull over when you hear sirens. What are you—from Russia or something?" This last sounded like a joke, so Brashnikov didn't reply.

Brashnikov felt the Tokarev pistol's cold butt under the cushions. He hated weapons, but Batenin had insisted he carry one when he was not in the suit. He

hoped he would not have to kill the man. Rair
Brashnikov considered himself a thief, not a murderer.

"Are you *militsiya*?" Brashnikov asked loudly. "Are
you cop? Show me badge. I want proof."

Then he got a good look at the running man's face.
The dead flat eyes over high cheekbones. It was the
one who had chased him from LCF-Fox. The one who
had the old Asian with him. How was this possible?

"Are you gonna stop or do I have to get rough?"
the man growled.

That was enough for Rair Brashnikov. He dared not
stop the car. There would not be enough time to don
the helmet and battery. The man's threat obviously
meant that he was armed. Otherwise, how could he
stop a speeding Cadillac?

The Tokarev came up in Rair's hand, crossing his
chest.

"Please," Brashnikov said. "Go away. I do not wish
to shoot you dead."

"Naughty, naughty," the man said, grabbing for the
half-open window. "Handguns are illegal in this state."

Brashnikov steeled himself and pulled the trigger.

The Tokarev did not fire. But it went off. It went
off Brashnikov's trigger finger as if pulled by a mag-
net. It left a long streak of blood along Brashnikov's
finger where the trigger guard had scraped the skin.

Sucking on his stinging finger, Brashnikov tried to
keep the wheel steady with his free hand. The road
was beginning to twist and turn. Brashnikov cast frightened glances at the still-running man.

He was busily taking the Tokarev to pieces. The
ammo clip came out and was thrown away. Then the
slide was yanked back in obviously strong fingers,
because it fell away. The long barrel was then un-
screwed like a light bulb. Finally the running man
broke the handle and firing mechanism into fragments,
and he dry-washed his hands clean of the metal filings

that were all that was left of the well-engineered Russian pistol.

All the while, he kept up the childish police-siren sound.

"Last chance to pull over," he warned.

Brashnikov rolled up the window and floored the gas pedal. He left the man behind when the engine started redlining.

But only for a moment. Because, incredibly, the running man in black began overhauling the Cadillac again, which was now skating up to the ninety-mile-an-hour mark.

The man in black was a red-lit phantom in the rearview mirror. Brashnikov nervously watched him come on. His running motions were hypnotic. It didn't look as if he was really running. The coordinated actions of his arms and legs were slow, floating motions. There was a distinct rhythm to his running. Then, abruptly, he shifted left and drew up alongside the spinning right-rear tire.

Craning to see, Brashnikov saw him pause in mid-step as if to kick out.

Brashnikov sent the Cadillac swerving. The man swerved with it, as if anticipating the car's every nervous move.

That lunatic is trying to kick my tire, Brashnikov thought wildly. For some reason the absurdity of it was lost on him. He hugged the shoulder of the highway, fearing what would happen next.

Rair heard the explosive sound of a blowout and then he was wrestling with the steering wheel as the hard rim of the wheel dug into the flattened rubber. It was incredible. The tire was flat. The Cadillac started to weave and lose speed.

While Rair Brashnikov fought the wheel, his mind racing, a car roared in from the right. It was a small European job, and it sideswiped him viciously, sending the Cadillac veering raggedly. Brashnikov turned around to see who was driving.

It was the red-haired woman. The one who had tried to knock him down with a helicopter back in North Dakota.

"Pull over," she was shouting. "Pull over, dammit, or I'll run you off the road." She flashed a photo-ID card, which was laughable. Did she think a KGB agent would be impressed by such a thing?

Then the running man with the toes of steel appeared on his right. He was shouting too. Not at him, but at the woman.

"Hey, cut it out," he told her.

"Get out of the way, you fink," she shot back. "I'm going to run this sucker off the road."

"Are you crazy?" the man yelled back. "His car is bigger than yours. You'll be killed. Let me handle this."

Telephone poles flashed by on either side of them. The road was narrowing and the wobbling Cadillac dominated it. The man hugged the Cadillac's right while the woman's tiny car wove in and out on the left.

"Don't tell me my job!" the redhead was insisting. "And get out of the way. How can I run him off the road with you there? How are you doing that, anyway? I'm pushing fifty."

"If I tell you, will you get lost?" the man asked.

"No," the redhead said flatly.

"Then forget it."

Rair Brashnikov could not accept the evidence of his ears anymore. They were fighting like children. Did Americans not take their national security seriously?

But Brashnikov's wonder vanished when he realized that he had his own skin to think of. Seeing the road ahead veer into a sharp turn, he saw a way to rid himself of both pursuers.

As the two vehicles and one running man hit the curve at fifty-three miles an hour, Brashnikov turned sharply to crowd the redhead's car. She met his challenge, crowding him back. But the Cadillac's flat tire made Brashnikov's machine more difficult to push. It didn't give, and when he realized this, he muscled the wheel sharply to the left.

Robin Green knew she wouldn't make the corner. She realized it too late. She hadn't been watching the road. She saw the telephone pole too late. It was framed in her windshield before her brain caught up with what her eyes were seeing and signaled "telephone pole in road." By then the windshield was already a splinterwork of cracks and the hood of the car was buckling like tinfoil and she could feel the seat pushing her forward and the wheel slamming into her chest.

The last thing she felt was her breasts. They felt like water balloons about to burst from impact.

Remo saw Robin Green's car pile into the telephone pole. It hit with so much force, it pushed the pole several feet beyond its posthole. A tangle of transmission lines slapped the buckled hood.

Remo forgot about the Cadillac and ran to the mangled wreck. Flames began licking up from under the hood like red fingers. The smell of roasting wood filled the air. As Remo thought of Robin trapped behind the wheel, the smell was a sickening premonition. He got to the driver's side. Robin was just there, her head slumped over the warped steering wheel. Her eyes were closed. There was a streak of blood across her forehead.

Remo grabbed the door handle. It was one of those reach-under-and-pull-up types. Remo pulled straight out. The handle came away like an oversize staple.

"Damn," Remo muttered. He looked for another

way in as the stench of flowing gasoline hit his nose like a chemical punch. He could see gas pooling under the rear bumper, away from the licking flames. But not for long. Already tendrils of gas were reaching out in all directions like feelers.

The driver's-side window was intact. But Remo knew if he shattered it, glass would fly into the car interior with dangerous consequences. Feeling his way around the door edge, Remo fervently wished cars still had external hinges. It would have been simpler to shear them off and pluck the door away. But this door was jammed shut.

Remo was about to hop across the hood to try the other side, when he noticed a hairline crack atop the window. It was not fully closed. He slipped his steel-hard fingers up under the rubber sealing strip and found the top of the glass. He levered down, and there came the grinding of an electric motor being forced into reverse as Remo pushed the window inexorably down against all manufacturers' recommendations.

When he had it halfway down, Remo reached in and shattered the exposed glass with a hard inside punch, sending jagged chunks out into the dirt. He pulled the door free and snapped Robin's seat belt. She didn't move. Her legs were wedged under the bent steering wheel, and Remo wondered if they were broken. He was about to check when a sudden *whoosh!* told him the fire had found the fuel in the engine. Now he had no choice.

Remo pulled Robin's limp body from behind the wheel as gently as he dared. Cradling her in his strong arms, he ran. He could feel the intensity of the flames building. The heat was on his back. When he knew the car was about to go, he dropped to his knees and shielded Robin's body with his own.

The car exploded like a cardboard box filled with skyrockets. Fire burst out of the windows, melting the tires and congealing glass. The upholstery burned with an acrid stink.

After the shock wave had passed, Remo looked back at the blazing ruin. No explosion-borne pieces of metal had landed near them. He looked down at Robin's pale face. Touching her temple, he felt the throbbing of her pulse. She looked almost angelic in the crackling backglow of the flames. For a moment Remo forgot her abrasive personality and saw her only as a gorgeous, desirable woman. He instantly regretted leaving her in the lurch back in North Dakota. When she awoke, Remo decided, he would apologize.

Robin Green's eyelids began fluttering and Remo tenderly wiped a thread of blood from her brow. It came from a minor cut near the hairline, he saw.

"Take it easy, kid," he whispered. "You're in safe hands."

The first words Robin spoke dispelled Remo's solicitous thoughts.

"That was a stupid macho thing you just did," she snapped. "I almost had him! He would have spilled his guts after two minutes with me."

"You tried to run him off the road, and you're calling *me* macho?" Remo said incredulously. "You were nearly killed, you know that?"

"Another minute and I would have had him."

"And I'm the Incredible Hulk," Remo said. "Here, give me your hand."

Robin pushed the offered hand away. "I can stand without help, thank you," she said frostily. Then she got up on wobbly knees. She fell back immediately, landing on her rump.

"I just need to catch my breath," she said in a weaker tone. "If only you hadn't interfered."

"Right," Remo said bitterly, looking down the long stretch of deserted highway. "If only I hadn't interfered."

"That guy would have pulled over in another minute," Robin Green insisted as she redid her buttons, which had come loose in the excitement. "Damn. I wish I had been born flat-chested."

"Be careful what you wish for," Remo said. "You might get it."

"Just what's that supposed to mean?"

Remo looked away.

"You hit that pole head-on," he said distantly. "You should be dead. You probably would have been if you hadn't had all that natural cushioning."

Robin followed the direction of Remo's gaze to the blazing tangle that was her car. She felt her breasts and winced. They hurt.

"Oh," she said in a shaken voice.

15

Robin Green was still very shaky when Remo pulled up in his rented car. He pushed open the door, and Robin eased herself into the passenger seat in obvious pain.

"Where's Charlie Chan?" Robin asked. "I thought you were going to fetch him."

"He wasn't there," Remo told her as he sent the car speeding down onto the road. "Just the car."

"Well, if you think I'm going to let you waste time chasing him down, you've got another think coming, buster," Robin snapped.

"Chiun wouldn't leave the car unless he saw something important. I think he spotted the *Krahseevah*."

"Fat lot of help he was," Robin said. "Where are you going?"

"After the *Krahseevah*," Remo told her. His dark eyes were intent on the road ahead.

"You can forget that too. He's long gone."

"A minute ago you were all hot to chase him. By the way, what are you doing here? Shouldn't you be in the brig or the stockade or whatever they call it?"

"The Air Force calls it corrective custody, and I have friends in high places. So I'm still on this case, no thanks to you."

"Me?" Remo said innocently. "What did I do?"

THE DESTROYER #78

"Do? You left me twisting in the wind, for one thing."

"Sorry. But I had my orders."

Remo spotted a fallen telephone pole and pulled over. He looked it over carefully, then started off again.

A few hundred yards down the highway, there was another felled pole, this time on the opposite side of the road.

"And that's another thing," Robin went on testily. "Who are you really? I've checked and the General Accounting Office never heard of you."

"Here," Remo said, handing her a photocard from his wallet. Robin took it.

"Remo Fleer, IRS," Robin read. Remo snatched the card away.

"Oops! Wrong card. Try this one."

"Remo Overn, OSI! Oh, give me a break."

"Hey, I'm undercover. Just like you. Or are you still with the OSI?"

"If you were OSI, you'd know that," Robin spat.

"Actually I've been pretty busy lately," Remo said airily. "Haven't kept up. I just noticed you were out of uniform and I wondered."

"That gives you away right there," Robin said triumphantly. "We only wear uniforms when we're undercover. No one knows who we are—even our rank is secret."

"Oh, yeah? What is your rank anyway? Major? Colonel? What?"

"None of your business."

"Maybe it's in these files," Remo said, taking a packet of folded sheets from his back pocket.

Robin, noticing that they were copies of her official OSI report on the first LCF-Fox incident, blew up.

"Where did you get these?" she said, grabbing them. "And don't feed me that crap about belonging to the

OSI. If either of us is caught with these, our goose is cooked."

"Oh, I have my ways," Remo said casually, retrieving his ID card. "Just like I'm going to find the *Krahseevah*."

"No chance. The trail's cold by now."

"Not to me. Want me to let you off somewhere?"

"You're not ditching me now."

"Look," Remo said seriously. "You've just come through a serious accident. You're at the very least banged up. You're certainly in no shape to play tag with this guy. So why don't I let you off somewhere where you can get medical treatment? It's for your own good."

"I can't. If I don't produce results, my plans will go up in smoke."

"What plans?" Remo wanted to know.

Robin fell silent. She leafed through the OSI files.

"Come on, what plans?" Remo prompted.

"If I crack this thing, maybe they'll let me join the Air Force for real," Robin admitted quietly.

Remo pulled over to the side of the road. "Hold the phone," he said. "You mean you're a fake?"

"No," Robin said levelly. She paused, took a breath, and went on shakily. "I've never admitted this to anyone before. I'm a service brat. Daddy didn't have any boys. Just me. I tried to enlist, to continue the family tradition."

"No go, huh?" Remo said sympathetically.

"I was rejected for a real chickenshit reason. They called it 'weight not in proportion to height.' The fatuous jerks!"

"Why not try again? You look pretty trim now."

"They weren't talking about my weight."

Remo frowned. "Then what—?"

"These aren't falsies, buster," Robin snapped, patting her breasts. "They're not detachable before induction physicals."

"Oh," Remo said, starting the car again. "That explains it."

"Damn straight it does."

"I meant the way you've been acting. Sensitive. Defensive. Trying to prove yourself. It all makes sense now. So how were you able to pass yourself off as an OSI agent?"

"I am *not* passing myself off," Robin insisted. "I *am* OSI. They employ civilian agents too. I passed *their* damn physical with no sweat. I turned out to be a damn good special agent and my record was spotless until this mess started. Now all I want is a chance to keep it clean. Then maybe—just maybe—they'll loosen up their silly regs so I can wear the uniform officially, not just when I'm undercover. If only I hadn't been cursed with these monster knockers."

"If you hadn't," Remo said dryly, "your face would right now be decorating the windshield of that wreck back there."

Robin had no answer to that.

"Tell you what," Remo said finally. "You do me a favor and I'll let you tag along until we catch this guy. Maybe we can work it so you get some of the credit."

"What do I have to do?" Robin asked in a wary voice.

"Simple," Remo said with a smile. "Just eat those reports."

"I beg your pardon?"

"You heard me. I was supposed to do it myself, but I forgot. They're perfectly digestible. Even the ink."

"You're joking."

"Take it or leave it. There's a town coming up ahead. I'll just drop you off at a gas station."

Robin looked at the files in her hand and then at Remo's sober profile. She examined the files again. She nibbled on a corner experimentally. She swallowed. Her expression was quizzical.

"How about you take half and I take half?" Robin suggested.

Remo thought about it. "Fair enough," he said. He put out his hand. They shook on it and then divided up Smith's files.

When they were done, Remo asked, "Now, that wasn't so bad, was it?"

"Not enough ink," Robin muttered. "You said you had a way of finding the *Krahseevah*."

"See that telephone pole we just passed?"

"No."

"That's because it's lying on its side. That's the fifth toppled pole we've gone by."

"And?"

"You know how Indians used to snap branches to leave trails through the forest? Chiun is leaving a trail for me to follow."

"The little guy did that?" Robin said, pointing to a dramatically leaning telephone pole coming up on their right.

"Without even trying. My guess is he spotted the *Krahseevah* while you were playing chicken and took off after him."

"And I suppose he just happened to forget to bring his car along?"

"Chiun doesn't like cars much. He says they're too slow."

"I'll believe it when I see it," Robin said huffily, folding her arms. She winced. Her ribs hurt. And her breasts felt like two humongous throbbing bruises.

Noticing her reaction, Remo asked, "You think you're up for this?"

"I'll be fine once I catch that Russian."

The lights of a desert community appeared up ahead. And in the solemn glow, a palm tree abruptly shook, shivered, and fell over.

"We're getting close," Remo said, pushing the accelerator to the limit.

*   *   *

Rair Brashnikov slowed down when he approached the town. Once he had changed his flat tire, he did not plan to stop again until he reached Los Angeles International Airport, but neither did he wish to attract the attention of the California authorities by driving too fast.

A neon sign on the left side of the road caught his eye. It said "Orbit Room Motel." As Rair drove past it, he saw that it was a low stucco building with an attached bar. The bar was dark but in the window rows of fine liquor bottles gleamed invitingly. Good American liquor was at a premium on the Russian black market.

Rair drove more slowly. Checking the rearview mirror, he saw no sign of pursuit.

He executed a careful U-turn and pulled into the Orbit Room parking lot, thinking: What harm could there be in it?

The Master of Sinanju left the palm toppled and sprinted on down the highway toward the lights of a town. He hoped that Remo was behind him. He could not understand what had happened to him.

Back at the place where they had waited for the *Krahseevah*, Chiun had been sitting in the car, his eyes keen and unwavering. He did not see the *Krahseevah* enter the building that for some reason was called by whites a plant, and did not see him leave it.

But it happened that his magnificent eyes spied his pupil, Remo, atop a building away from his post. Chiun recognized from Remo's crouching body language that he was stalking someone.

That was enough for the Master of Sinanju, who burst from the car like a blot of blackness. He circled the building, searching with his eyes.

The faint glow of the *Krahseevah* became visible crossing an open stretch of highway. Hearing the sound of a car motor start up, Chiun knew that the Russian was going to attempt escape by vehicle.

Seeing Remo sprint for the car, Chiun decided that Remo had the situation in hand. But just in case, he would take the low road and be prepared to join Remo in the chase.

Chiun waited in the middle of the road, his sleeves linked, his face resolute, for the big car to turn the corner.

It never did. Instead, its headlight glow swept above Chiun's head and past him. The Cadillac had taken the ridge road.

Annoyed that Remo had allowed this to happen, Chiun flounced around and, sandals slapping the black-top silently, streaked after it. He stayed on the low road, knowing that the two roads ran parallel for several miles before diverging.

When the ridge road flattened, Chiun saw the Cadillac moving rapidly. There was no sign of Remo. Chiun frowned. What could have happened to him?

Chiun crossed over a strip of desert to the other road and fell in behind the Cadillac. He maintained a decorous pace, keeping the car's taillights always in view, but never allowing his night-black kimono to be visible. Every few hundred yards he paused to fell a telephone pole.

Now the Cadillac was slowing as it came to the city limits. Dawn was turning the east pinkish-orange.

And as Chiun rounded a turn in the road, he saw the Cadillac pull into a combination motel/bar called the Orbit Room Motel.

Chiun dropped to a trot, and his arms ceased their steady pumping. He glanced over his shoulder. But there was still no sign of Remo. It was puzzling.

As Chiun drew up to the neon Orbit Room sign, he was no longer running. He was flitting from mailbox to palm tree, a patch of shadow that no human eye could perceive.

Chiun saw the *Krahseevah* leave the big car. He wore an overcoat so that only his white boots showed. He carried the car battery and the collapsed bladder-like helmet under one arm. The tiles were not in his possession. He went around to the back of the bar.

Chiun drifted up to the Cadillac. He peered into the interior. There was a cardboard box in the back seat. The door was locked, but that did not deter the Master of Sinanju. He tapped his fingernails against the rear window. He tapped steadily, insistently, until the glass suddenly radiated cracks. It crystallized into nuggetlike pieces. Laying his palm against it, Chiun pushed in the window glass like a piece of soft cardboard. It plopped onto the seat with a mushy sound.

Chiun extricated the cardboard box and undid the flaps. The box contained over a dozen black tiles. Pleased, Chiun took the box to a mailbox and sent it sliding down the chute for safekeeping. He did not want them damaged in the conflict to come.

Then he marched for the front door of the bar. He vowed to himself that this time he would leave no walls for the *Krahseevah* to conceal himself in.

Remo almost drove past the Orbit Room Motel without noticing the parked Cadillac.

He finally spotted it when he executed a sharp U-turn and pulled into the parking lot.

"I hope this doesn't mean what I think it means," Robin Green said unhappily. She was looking at the motel's stucco face. Or rather, what was left of it.

For the Orbit Room Motel looked like a piece of white cheese that had been nibbled on by rats. Scablike chunks were falling from great holes even as Remo pulled into a spot. When he got out, his car door banged the one parked next to his. Remo noticed that it was a Cadillac. He checked the rear license plate. It matched the number of the *Krahseevah*'s machine.

But Remo didn't have time to consider that. He had spotted the Master of Sinanju.

Chiun leapt from a gaping cavity in the stucco corner. Whirling, he attacked the face of the building, his long fingernails working like scores of high-speed clippers. Stucco flew like broken teeth.

From the entrance, hotel personnel and guests in their nightclothes and underwear poured out screaming. They piled into cars and drove off in a mass exodus of confusion.

"Chiun, hold up," Remo called.

The Master of Sinanju turned, his clawlike hands poised.

"Remo! What kept you? Never mind. Come help me. The white thing is inside this building. We must root him out." And Chiun slashed a long horizontal line across the cracked stucco as he ran the length of the building's face.

"You'd better stay here," Remo told Robin in a solicitous tone. "Okay?"

"Are you kidding?" she said. "I had a tough enough time explaining one wreck of a hotel without being involved in another."

"Good girl," Remo said, starting off.

Robin watched him go. "What am I thinking?" she said, cocking her automatic. "He's going to blow it again." She squeezed out and limped after Remo.

When Remo stepped up behind Chiun, the Master of Sinanju turned on him, his face furious.

"Do not merely stand there like useless baggage," he shrieked. "I have followed that dastard here, no thanks to you, and I— "

Chiun's hazel eyes narrowed at the sight of Robin Green limping up.

"How did she get here?" he hissed explosively.

"I pulled some strings," Robin informed him.

Chiun blinked. "Strings?" he asked, approaching her. "Tell me of these strings. Are they part of the blue smoke and mirrors? I do not remember you saying 'blue smoke, mirrors, and strings.' What kind of string is employed?"

"What's he jabbering about?" Robin asked Remo.

"Look, let's save this for our old age, shall we?" Remo said. He turned to Chiun. "You say the *Krahseevah*'s inside? Fine. Let's dig him out and we'll sort out the pieces later."

Robin Green opened her mouth to say something, but her gaze was caught by something above and behind them. Her mouth froze in the open position.

Remo and Chiun turned just in time to see the *Krahseevah*'s featureless face emerge from the stucco wall above their heads.

Robin sent two rounds into its face. Two spiderweb holes shattered the textured stucco. The face withdrew.

"It's on the second floor," she yelled.

Remo grabbed her gun.

"No wild shooting," he hissed. "We don't know if there are still people up there."

"Not after your friend, the Eastern earthquake, started in on this place," Robin said.

"I resent that," Chiun said.

"Both of you just put it away. C'mon, let's hit the second floor."

They went in together. The lobby was deserted. At Remo's suggestion, they split up. Robin followed him up a flight of stairs. Chiun took the elevator.

They reached the second floor simultaneously. Virtually every door was wide open, thanks to the mass evacuation caused by Chiun's attempt to bring the hotel down around the *Krahseevah*'s head.

"This should be easy," Remo said as he passed from door to door.

"Look," Robin put in, pointing to a closed door. "Care to bet if he's in that room?"

"You're covered," Remo said. "Come on."

"Can I have my weapon back?" Robin whispered as they closed in on the door.

"No," Remo and Chiun said in different degrees of vehemence.

Rair Brashnikov knew he had a problem. He could easily slip out of the hotel in his incorporeal state, but he could not drive off without turning off the suit. He knew from his experiences with the white man and the little Oriental that they were more than human. It was very strange. They possessed no electronic augmentation, but they did things no human could possibly accomplish. They would follow him no matter where he went, tireless and inexhaustible—which was more than Rair could say for the battery pack that powered his vibration suit. It was advertised as a sixty-month battery, good for over five hundred cold cranking amps for all-weather starts. But that guarantee held only if it was hooked up to a car. The suit usually drained it after twelve hours' continuous use.

There was only one thing to do. He turned off the suit and picked up the room telephone. He hit the outside-line button, and got a dial tone. Quickly Brashnikov dialed the Soviet-embassy number he had carefully committed to memory now that it represented his ultimate trump card in the game of espionage.

The phone rang. Once, twice. Then the door crashed open and Rair Brashnikov reached for the belt rheostat, steeling himself for the ordeal of fiberoptic cable teleportation.

They all saw the *Krahseevah*, his outline sharp and clear, poised, receiver in hand.

"Got him!" Remo exulted.

"No, he is mine!" Chiun cried.

They both swept into the room like black-clad demons.

Then the *Krahseevah* touched his belt. His sharp

outlines blurred. He glowed like the moon seen through fog.

Then, a strange thing happened. The *Krahseevah*'s blurred outlines shifted and wavered. Remo was almost upon him when it happened.

The *Krahseevah* congealed like a luminous mist. It collapsed, and, like smoke, was drawn into the hovering receiver. It looked like a special-effects film run in reverse. The last bit of him to go was the hand that held the receiver. When that was gone, the telephone plummeted to the rug.

Remo caught it, one step ahead of Chiun.

Robin screamed.

"Oh, my God," she cried. "What happened to it?"

Remo, his eyes staring, looked at the receiver with a dumbfounded expression.

"It was sucked into the phone," Remo said slowly. "I think."

"Oh, do not be ridiculous," Chiun snapped.

"You got a better explanation?" Remo retorted.

"It was like he was made of smoke," Robin said in a stunned voice.

"Hah!" exclaimed Chiun. "Then there is truth behind those inscrutable words, blue smoke and mirrors. Now, where are the mirrors? I see no mirrors. Or string."

Remo put the receiver to his ear experimentally. There was a great deal of static, but through it he heard a voice. A Russian voice. It was saying, "Oh, no, not again! Brashnikov, you idiot!"

Then the Russian voice screamed and Remo heard a flurry of frantic shouting and activity.

Seeing Remo's absurd expression, Chiun demanded, "What is it? What do you hear?"

"Russians. I think the *Krahseevah*'s in the line somewhere."

"He will not escape us so easily," Chiun declared,

leaping to the baseboard. He began pulling the telephone wire free like string from soft butter.

"No, Chiun," Remo said, stopping him. "Hold up. We've got an open line here, let's not lose it." He handed Chiun the receiver. "Here, you keep listening."

Remo plunged into the next room, got an outside line, and called Dr. Harold W. Smith.

Smith's answer was sleepy.

"Remo. What is it?"

"Can you trace a line for us?"

"Yes, of course. One moment, I'm speaking from my briefcase phone. Let me take it to the next room, where I won't wake my wife."

A moment later, the sound of Smith keying his portable briefcase computer came to Remo's ears. Swiftly Remo gave him the hotel name and the room number the *Krahseevah* had used.

"It's the Soviet embassy again," Smith told him after a long silence.

"Well, I've got good news and bad news for you, then."

"What's the bad?"

"The *Krahseevah* got away from us again. And I know how freaky this is going to sound, but you'll have to take it on faith. He got away through the phone system."

"We must have a bad connection, Remo. I thought you just said—"

"I did," Remo said, cutting him off. "He was holding an open line, turned on the suit, and he was gone like a milkshake through a drinking straw. Into the receiver."

There was a long silence over the line. It hissed.

"There is no way you could have been deceived?" Smith demanded at last. "No chance of trickery or optical illusion?"

"No. I saw it. Chiun saw it. And Robin saw it."

"Robin Green?" Smith's voice was sharp. "How did she get there?"

"Good question. I forgot to ask. Anyway, I think we'd better go after the embassy people."

"No. Emphatically, no. You said something about good news."

"Oh, yeah. The *Krahseevah* didn't have the tiles with him when he got sucked away. I don't know where they are, but he didn't have them."

"They are in the mail," Chiun called from the next room.

"Smitty, Chiun just said they're in the mail." Remo listened a moment. He put his hand over the mouthpiece. "Hey, Chiun. Smith wants to know if you addressed them to him."

"No. I simply put them in a postal box."

"Oh. Hear that, Smitty? . . . Sure, I'll get them back. So what do we do now?"

"Return to Folcroft," Smith said after a pause. "We are facing incredible technology and we must stop it now."

"Okay. We'll ditch Robin somehow."

"No. Bring her. But make certain she sees nothing that will provide her with a trail back to CURE."

"Gotcha," Remo said, hanging up.

The first thing Robin Green said to Remo when he returned to the other room was, "Who is Smith?"

"Look," Remo said, raising his hands. "Do us both a big favor. Pretend you never heard the name Smith. Okay?"

"Not okay. I asked you a direct question. Who is Smith and what does he have to do with you two?"

"Listen, I'm telling you that you'll be a lot better off if you don't know. Just, please, don't mention his name to his face, okay?"

"To his face? Is he coming here?"

"No, we're going to see him."

"I'm not going anywhere without some answers first."

"Sorry," Remo said, edging closer. "I have my orders."

Robin Green quickly backed away. "Wait a minute, buster. You just keep your chicken-plucking hands away from me."

"Quickly, Remo," Chiun put in unconcernedly. "I wish to leave immediately."

"Give me a sec, okay? Look, I'm sorry," Remo said to Robin, cornering her by a window. "This won't hurt a bit."

"Hurt! Wait! Don't do anything you'll be sorry for later. My father is a full bird colonel. If you so much as lay a hand on me, he'll hunt you down. He'll—"

Remo reached out and squeezed a nerve in her neck. Robin Green's eyes rolled up into her head. She exhaled a slow, summery sigh and slumped into Remo's arms. He carried her easily.

"Excellent," Chiun said as he breezed out of the room. "Thus we will not have to listen to her on the trip back to Folcroft."

"Did you catch what she said about her father?" Remo asked as they took the elevator down. "No wonder she's not up on charges. Her father's been protecting her."

"And it is no wonder that she is named Robin," Chiun sniffed. "With a father who is a bird. What kind of depraved woman must her mother have been?"

16

Robin Green's vision cleared slowly. At first, everything was a blur. Her arms felt stiff. When she breathed, she inhaled her own exhaust. She felt enclosed, claustrophobic. And her ears rang, just like they would after a long flight.

"Better get set," a familiar voice said through the ringing. "Looks like she's coming to."

Into her blurred brown field of vision moved a vertical column of gray. It stopped before her. A man, she decided.

Robin tried to speak, but her throat was clogged. She coughed to clear it. Her eyes watered. Surprisingly, that seemed to help. The gray blur grew more distinct.

Robin realized that she was sitting down. There was a strange cottonlike smell in her nose. She squeezed her hands, but couldn't feel them. Panic started to mount in her throat. Had she been injured in the car accident more than she thought? Had any of the events that followed it actually happened?

She clutched at herself. Her breasts felt tender. She remembered the smashed steering wheel.

"Can you hear me?" she asked the gray blur.

"Yes," replied a male voice, dry and bitter as a week-old lemon peel. "Please do not exert yourself until the bandages are removed."

Robin gasped involuntarily. "Bandages? Am I okay?"

"Sure," another voice said from behind her. "The X rays were all negative. Now, just sit still a minute." It was that first voice. Remo whatever-his-name-was.

Then it all came back in a rush of memory. The car crash. The fight at the motel. Remo's hand reaching out to her, and then . . . oblivion.

"What . . . what did you do to me?" she sobbed, reaching for her face. She couldn't feel her face. She couldn't even feel her fingertips. They were swathed in fabric. Or was it her face? Then her vision cleared.

Robin realized she was in a small room. The walls were odd. Not covered with paint or wallpaper, but Naugahyde or something similar. Like overstuffed upholstery. Padded and . . . Padded . . .

"Oh, God," she gasped. "I'm in a padded cell."

Then she saw the man. He was all in gray. A handheld mirror shielded his face. The mirror side reflected Robin's own face. It was the face of a Hollywood mummy. Only her stark and staring blue eyes showed through the winding gauze.

"Please calm yourself," the gray man said from behind the mirror. "The procedure is quite painless, I can assure you."

Robin felt a strong hand—presumably Remo's—take the top of her head, and the tiny snippings of surgical scissors began. She looked down and saw her bandaged hands clutching the armrests of a chair.

"Am I . . .?" Robin choked out. "Will I be . . . disfigured?"

"Nah," Remo said. "The bandages were so we could get you onto the airline flight while you were unconscious."

"What?" Robin barked indignantly.

"I asked Remo to bring you here," the gray man said. "It was necessary that you not see anything that could lead you back to Remo or myself. You were transported as a catatonic burn patient."

"Smith! Are you Smith?" Robin demanded. "Because if you are, you're in big trouble, buster."

The gray man gasped involuntarily. "Remo," he said in a shocked voice.

"Sorry, Smitty. Your name slipped out. But don't worry. Robin's on our side."

"The hell I am," Robin shouted. Suddenly the bandages fell away. Her mouth hung open. Her reflection stared back at her. Except for a few bruises and a cut near her hairline, it was normal—if paler than usual. She breathed a sigh of relief.

"See?" Remo said brightly, coming around the front. "Good as new."

"Step aside," Robin told him acidly. "I want to talk with your boss."

"And we want to talk with you," the man Robin took for Smith said matter-of-factly. "So please try to calm yourself."

"Calm myself!" Robin cried, pushing herself from the chair. "This loon just kidnapped me. I'm an Air Force investigator. You can't get away with this crap."

"Allow me, Emperor," a squeaky voice said from behind her left ear. And a hand with long curved fingernails reached up behind her hair and took the nape of her neck.

Robin felt her legs suddenly go numb, as if they had gone to sleep. She fell back into the chair.

"What is this?" she demanded. And then she noticed for the first time that she was sitting in a wheelchair.

"Oh, dear Lord," she said weakly, the fight going out of her.

"The paralysis is only temporary," Smith told her. "Chiun will restore the use of your legs after we have the answers we seek."

Chiun stepped into view, his face placid.

"You bastard," she hissed at him. And the old Oriental's face took on an injured expression.

"Perhaps if you continue to insult me, I will forget how to realign your spine," Chiun warned her.

"He doesn't mean that," Remo put in quickly.

"Yes, I do," Chiun snapped.

"Please, please," Smith said. "Miss Green, if you will just answer my questions, we can be done with this interview."

"Why don't you put down that stupid mirror first? I can see that my face is fine, thank you."

"This mirror is not for your benefit," Smith told her. "It is so that you cannot see my face for later identification."

"Then could you please turn it around? You can stare at your own face for a change."

"This is a two-way mirror. I can see you from this end. If I turn it around, my features will be visible to you."

At that, Chiun sidled up to Smith, his face craning up at the mirror. He examined it from front and rear. "May I borrow that when you are through with it?" he asked curiously. "It may be what I have been looking for."

"Later," Smith said testily.

"What do you want to know?" Robin said quietly, her face flushed.

"How did you happen to be on the scene when the *Krahseevah*, as Remo has styled him, reappeared?"

"You know, I could ask the same of you."

"Simply answer the question."

"All right. Did Remo—if that's really his name—tell you about the gas-station owner who saw the guy without his helmet?"

"Yes," Smith said, voice puzzled.

"Well, after I was ditched by your friends, I had a hard time explaining the demolished Holiday Inn, but fortunately, I have friends in high places."

"We know your father has been protecting you. He's been informed that you are well and not to worry. And just to be certain we have no problems from that quarter, I had him shipped off to a NATO base in Europe. He will not interfere."

"Oh," Robin said, subsiding. She swallowed and went on. "Anyway, strings were pulled and I was allowed to stay on the case. I rounded up Ed, the gas-station owner, his brother Ned, and the Holiday Inn desk clerk and had them describe the Russian's face for an artist I hired. We came up with a great likeness. Since then, we've had Air Force personnel watching airports and train stations all over the country. When someone who looked like our guy showed up at Los Angeles International Airport, I flew out there. I tracked him as far as the Northrop plant. Then he slipped into the suit and got away from me. I kept his car under surveillance, waiting for him to return. When he took off, I took off after him." She turned to glare at Remo. "I would have had him, too, but Remo Roadrunner here screwed things up."

"Me?" Remo said hotly. "I was on his tail first. You're a Robin-come-lately as far as I'm concerned."

"That's it?" Smith asked in a disappointed voice. "That's the lead you followed?"

Robin defiantly shook red hair out of her eyes. "What did you expect? That he called, asked for a date, and gave me his phone number?"

"That much we know," Smith said dryly. "He operates out of the Soviet embassy in Washington."

"Well, back to square one," Remo said. "Sorry, Smitty. I thought she'd have a better story than that."

"I thought it was a pretty sound piece of investigation," Robin muttered. "Why didn't any of you think of it?"

"She's got us there, Smitty," Remo admitted.

"Never mind," Smith said.

"Look," Robin said. "This was my investigation before it was yours. I know you guys aren't what you claim to be. I can live with that. But thanks to Punch and Judy over there"—Robin indicated Remo and Chiun with a disdainful toss of her head—"I'm probably AWOL from the scene of yet another demolished hotel. If I don't bag this *Krahseevah*, my career has flown south forever. Help me, and I'll help you. I'm in so deep even my father can't pull me out of this mess."

"We do not need you," Chiun told her pointedly. "You, who think that blue smoke and mirrors can explain anything your feeble mind cannot trouble itself to understand."

Robin just stared at the Master of Sinanju uncomprehendingly.

"We have recovered the RAM tiles," Smith said slowly. "There is a chance that the *Krahseevah* will return to Palmdale, but it's doubtful he would dare to anytime in the near future. He knows we would expect that. Given his past pattern of infiltration and theft, he could strike anywhere in our military-industrial complex. We cannot afford to wait. He must be captured and neutralized as soon as possible."

Remo stepped forward. "But how, Smitty?" he said. "It was bad enough when we just couldn't lay hands on him. But now that we know he can just dive into any handy telephone at the first sign of trouble, I don't see what even Chiun and I can do."

"I suggest we descend upon the Russian embassy," Chiun proclaimed loudly. "We will take hostages. We will force them to deliver the *Krahseevah* to us and then we will kill him and every other Russian as a warning to their leader not to send any more such as him to America's well-protected shores."

"No," Smith said. "The principle of diplomatic immunity is important to our side too. We cannot jeopardize that privilege. It is out of the question."

"What is this faintheartedness I am hearing?" Chiun asked Remo *sotto voce*. "Smith never used to be like this."

"Relations with Russia have warmed," Remo whispered back. "Smith doesn't want to rock the boat."

"I have been doing some research," Smith said carefully. "It seems that three years ago there was an event at a Nishitsu Corporation plant in Osaka. Several top physicists perished and the matter was hushed up. Prior to that there had been leaks from Nishitsu of an incredible superconductor breakthrough involving atomic matter. Not energy, but matter. If, as I suspect, this was a KGB 'wet-affairs' operation, we can deduce that the suit now in Soviet hands is not a product of their limited technology, but a Japanese prototype. In other words, I doubt there is another *Krahseevah* waiting in the wings."

"So if we capture our *Krahseevah*," Remo said, "the problem is solved. Right?"

"I assume so."

"But how? He's like the little man who wasn't there. We can see him, but we can't touch him."

"Except when the suit is off," Smith pointed out.

"Yeah. But he never has his hands far from his belt-buckle control. He sees us coming and he's covered."

"I have been thinking about this suit," Smith told them. "I believe I understand the telephone phenomenon. It is a kind of teleportation, which physicists have long theorized as possible. You, Remo, have described how the *Krahseevah* stuck his head out of the Palmdale motel to observe you. Yet he had the suit off moments later when he used the telephone. It was only when you arrived that he turned it back on."

"That's right," Remo admitted.

"We know we cannot touch him while the suit is on. The reverse, therefore, must be true. The *Krahseevah* has to turn the suit off before he can physically touch something he intends to steal. Then he must reactivate the suit, and the object somehow becomes, as he is, noncorporeal."

"What does his military rank have to do with this?" Chiun snapped, feeling left out of all this white mumbo-jumbo.

"He said 'noncorporeal.' Not 'noncorporal,' " Remo told him. "It means 'insubstantial.' "

"I knew that," Chiun said, not wishing to appear foolish. Why did these Americans have to have so many names for the same thing? he wondered. They were worse than the old Romans.

Smith went on. "If we know the *Krahseevah*'s next target, we can be waiting for him. In the few seconds the suit is not operating, either you, Remo, or Chiun might be able to take him. You're fast enough."

"Definitely," Chiun said with confidence.

"But how do we figure out where he's going to turn up next?" Robin wanted to know.

"We are going to set a trap for him," Smith told her. "And you, Miss Green, are going to be the bait."

And suddenly OSI Special Agent Robin Green wasn't as anxious to be freed from her wheelchair imprisonment as she had thought.

17

Major Yuli Batenin grabbed the edge of his desk when the phone rang. Even from beyond the closed door, the shrill, insistent sound went through him like a hot needle.

"Answer that damned thing!" he shouted into the intercom.

There was no telephone in Major Batenin's embassy office anymore. He had had the line removed to the reception area. Never again would Major Yuli Batenin answer a telephone as long as he lived. Not after what Brashnikov had done to him. Again.

It had not been as horrendous an experience, having Rair Brashnikov explode from the receiver a second time. At the warning roar of static, Batenin had thrown the receiver away and dived under his desk.

When he emerged, after the flash of white light faded, Brashnikov was not to be seen. Frantic, Batenin called in his staff and instituted a thorough search. The embassy was put on yellow alert. Every staff member, from the now-furious ambassador to the low-liest clerk, rushed about the embassy searching for him.

It was getting so that the existence of the vibration suit could not be kept secret much longer. Even the cleaning staff whispered about it.

They found Brashnikov in the office directly under Batenin's. Or rather, they found his feet.

For Rair Brashnikov's gold-veined white boots were sticking up from the floor as if cut off at the ankles and placed upside down by a ghoulish prankster. And of course, they were sinking into the floor.

This realization sent everyone scrambling down another floor, where they discovered Brashnikov hanging from the ceiling like a great white bat.

Brashnikov's face membrane was in an expanded position, Batenin saw. Then the red belt light winked on and half the staff cleared the room in mute panic. The half that stayed had not known the significance of the red light. Batenin took careful pains to explain it to them.

After he had finished, others began to edge toward the door. Batenin was about to warn them of the consequences of not obeying him, when someone pointed at Brashnikov.

Batenin turned. The face was silently contracting. Brashnikov was breathing. Batenin looked ceilingward and saw that Brashnikov's booted toes were just about to come free of the ceiling.

"Brashnikov," Batenin shouted at him. "Do not turn off suit. Do you understand me? Do not touch suit."

Brashnikov waved his arms feebly. Batenin couldn't tell if he had heard him.

Then the tip of his toes emerged from the ceiling. Batenin examined the toes from every angle before satisfying himself that they were not in contact with the plaster.

"Now, Brashnikov! Turn off suit now!"

Weakly Rair Brashnikov reached for his buckle. His hand twisted. Brashnikov's fuzzy outline clarified, and the suit came into hard focus. Rair Brashnikov landed on his head with a loud *thunk*.

Batenin rushed to the fallen man and pulled off his helmet, which came away with the ripping sound of separating Velcro.

"Brashnikov! Are you well?" demanded Batenin, who secretly hoped the stupid thief had broken his neck.

"*Da,*" Rair Brashnikov said feebly.

"You have Stealth tiles?"

Brashnikov shook his head dazedly. "*Nyet.* They found me again. The two I spoke of. I had to escape."

Hearing that, Yuli Batenin became a madman. He had to be pulled off Rair Brashnikov before he could strangle him. The thief's true face had turned a smoky lavender before Batenin's thick fingers were pried from Brashnikov's throat.

Now, a day later, Yuli Batenin sat in his phoneless office, worrying about the messages being telexed between Moscow and the Soviet ambassador. Twice he had failed to deliver the promised RAM tiles. He knew he could not honorably return to the Motherland until that last piece of Stealth technology was in his hands.

So when his secretary informed him that there was a call for him, Yuli Batenin pried his clenched fingers from the desk's edge and opened a drawer. He extracted a desktop speaker. It was wired to the reception-room line. Batenin had insisted on this after being assured by the technical-support person who maintained the vibration suit that there was no way that Brashnikov could emerge from a mere satellite speaker.

Just to be certain, he tripped the intercom. "Where is Brashnikov?" he demanded. Receiving assurances that the thief was recuperating in the infirmary, Batenin placed the speaker on his desk and turned it on.

"Yes?" he said, fearing the worst—a call from the Kremlin.

"You are the embassy's chargé d'affaires?" a saucy female voice asked in an unidentifiable American regional accent.

"Yes. Who is this, please?"

"I am an Air Force investigator who's had to go AWOL, thanks to your phantom thief."

"I do not understand."

"I was assigned to LCF-Fox. Your man made a monkey of me there, and again at the Northrop Stealth plant. Let's not pussyfoot around. I'm a dead duck as far as my superiors are concerned. There were too many unexplained thefts and no one believed me when I tried to tell them the truth."

"What truth?" Batenin asked cautiously.

"About the white ghost with no face."

"I am not following you," Batenin said vaguely.

"You can check my story if you want. See if a special agent Robin Green is AWOL from the OSI. You know what the OSI is?"

"No, but I can look it up. What are you suggesting?" he asked, having received such calls from disgruntled U.S. military personnel before. They always wanted one thing, and Batenin thought that the less they discussed Brashnikov over an open line, the better.

"Political asylum. And I have something to trade for it."

"And what is that?"

"A U.S. military device even your ghost cannot steal without help."

"Naturally, I have no idea what you talk about. Ghosts are for children's fairy tales."

"Be as cagey as you want," the female voice said, "but what I have to trade is very big. And your man can only steal it if he knows what it is and where to find it. And I can supply that in return for safe passage to Russia and the usual arrangements."

"You are talking about defecting, *nyet*?"

"I am talking about the best damn trade you'll ever get handed to you. If you have any contacts that can verify my rank and current status, do it. I'll call back in an hour."

In that hour, Yuli Batenin set his staff to work. In short order they verified the existence of an OSI special agent named Robin Green, who was in fact miss-

ing and presumed absent without leave. There were
several notations in her file that could not be explained. The matter of a half-demolished Holiday Inn
in North Dakota and another damaged motel in
Palmdale, California.

By the time the woman called back, Major Batenin
knew he had a very big fish.

"You are genuine," Yuli told her. "Perhaps."

"Where should we meet?" she asked him.

Batenin named a popular steakhouse in Washington, famous for its prime rib. He arrived ten minutes
late, and was led past the bar, where autographed
portraits of the restaurant's political clients covered
virtually every square inch of wall space.

He sat at a solitary table and ordered a gin and
tonic, but when it came he told the puzzled waitress
that he had made a mistake. He would prefer vodka.

At that remark, an attractive redhead with sparkling
blue eyes slid into the booth, facing him.

"You are Green?" he asked.

"Right at the moment, I'm black and blue. But
that's my name, all right. And you?"

"Call me Yuli," Batenin said, his dark eyes falling
to her chest. She wore a clingy knit dress that was cut
just low enough to display her ample cleavage. For a
passing moment Batenin wondered if this could be a
CIA sex trap. It was not uncommon. The KGB did it
to Americans. The CIA did it to Russians. It was a
game everyone played.

"I will provide nothing until you deliver," Yuli said
carefully, knowing that his diplomatic immunity would
safeguard him from arrest. And if this was a CIA trap,
what was the worst they could do? Declare him per-
sona non grata and ship him back to Moscow? This
was exactly what Batenin wanted.

"Agreed," Robin Green said, leaning closer. Her
perfume tickled his nostrils. "Now, listen carefully,"
she said after the vodka came and she waved the

waitress aside without ordering. "Your people are very anxious to obtain Stealth technology. No, I don't expect you to answer that. But I know that your spook— and I use the term advisedly—has been pilfering it hither and yon."

Batenin took a sip of his vodka. Headlights from a passing car threw the woman into sharp relief. It was then that Batenin decided that she could not be a CIA sex lure. Her face, under subtle makeup, showed bruises. Even her cleavage was a discolored yellowish-purple. She looked like she had been in a car wreck. He wondered what had happened to her.

"Okay," she went on, "you're probably aware that even with the first planes only now becoming public knowledge, the Stealth program is ten years old. By the time the Stealth bomber is fully operational, it's going to be obsolete. There's something new."

"I am listening," Batenin said coolly, taking another sip of his drink. His gaze raked the room. The other diners looked harmless. He sensed no eyes on him. He relaxed slightly.

"They've perfected the Stealth radar-absorbing material to a new plateau. Not just invisible to radar, this stuff is invisible, period. It's a transparent resin-based polymer mounted on a silicon-mica base. When it's pumped full of electricity, it is virtually invisible in flight. From a distance, you can't even make out the pilot or the engines. And best of all, it has all the radar-deflecting properties of existing Stealth material."

"This sounds, shall we say, preposterous?" Batenin said archly.

"No more preposterous than an electronic suit that will allow a man to walk through a solid wall," Robin countered. "Are you interested?"

"I must have more particulars. For my superiors."

"This stuff is so new, so experimental, that all the Air Force has now is a scale-model prototype. But it's operational. It's about to be shown to a secret con-

gressional committee. But until then they have it in a
nuclear-weapons storage bunker. It's supposed to be
impregnable, but your man should have no problem
with it."

"You have the exact location of this bunker?" Batenin
asked, his remote voice fluttering with the first hints of
real interest.

"It's Bunker Number 445. Pease Air Force Base,
Portsmouth, New Hampshire. It's going to be moved
within the next two days, so your man had better
move fast."

"How do I know this is not some inane American
trap?"

"Look, I'm going to assume you checked me out,
otherwise you wouldn't be here. So you know who I
am, and you know my butt is in a sling over your
agent's shenanigans. That means I know what he can
do. And I know, just as you do, that nothing—no
trap, no technology, no scheme—could possibly snare
him. Right?"

Yuli Batenin nodded silently, his eyes staring into
the distance. When they refocused, he said, "If this
works out, I can definitely offer you what you want.
Where can I reach you?"

"I'm hot," Robin Green said, rising to her feet. "So
I'm going to be on the move until you get me on a
plane. I'll check in periodically. Deal?"

"Done," said Yuli Batenin, who looked into the
woman's frank American eyes but saw instead the
lights of faraway Moscow.

18

Airman Henry Yauk thought it was ridiculous.

"What do you mean, no one's going to relieve us?" he asked his companion in the guard tower.

"That's the word," Sergeant Frank Dinan told him. "When we go off duty, we just go. We don't wait for relief and we don't hang around either."

"We just leave the nukes unguarded, is that it?" Yauk said angrily.

"That's it."

"Unbelievable. I know the base is being phased out, but isn't this a little premature?"

"Search me," Dinan said. He was looking out over the bunkers. Darkness had fallen. It was a warm Indian-summer night in New Hampshire. Moonlight brushed the grass-covered tops of the nuclear-weapons storage bunkers so that they looked like sleeping silver-furred monsters.

"I wonder if this has anything to do with opening up Number 445?" Yauk muttered.

"Search me," Dinan said again. Yauk frowned. He hated being paired with Dinan. The guy was a bogus conversationalist.

"I never saw them put a nuke back into a bunker like that. No special-purpose vehicle. No guards. Just a civilian truck."

Dinan said nothing. Yauk looked at his watch. His

frown deepened. Five more minutes until the end of their shift.

For as long as Airman Yauk had been an SP at Pease Air Force Base, the nuclear-weapons bunkers had never been unguarded. Officially, there were no nukes stored at Pease, even though it was a SAC bomber base, headquarters of the 509th Bombardment Wing. At any given time, five fully manned FB-111 bombers sat under open-ended hangars on the flight line, ready to be cart-started in the event of a nuclear war, cocked nuclear bombs cradled in their bays. Everybody knew that. Just as everybody knew that the twin rows of bunkers hunched behind the wire-link fences were nuclear-weapons storage containers.

Few civilians ever saw these bunkers, however, which was why the base public-affairs officer was able to keep a straight face whenever he was forced to categorically deny the official Air Force line that absolutely no nuclear weapons were quartered at Pease. The bunkers looked like prehistoric turtles that had died, their heads drawn into their shells and the grass of ages grown over their sloping sides. The grass was to prevent the bunkers from being indentifiable from the air. This, of course, was a joke. From the air it would look like the Air Force had fenced off a section of the base and set a solitary guard tower around it just so SP's like Airman Yauk could keep gophers off official Air Force grass.

A utility road ran past the fence. Beyond it, a solitary road paralleled it. This road looped around the boarded-up Sportsman's Club and came back. This was so if any suspicious car drove past the security fence, it would have no place to go except back the way it had come, where it would be intercepted.

And although there were signs posted on the fence that warned that the SP's in the towers were authorized to use lethal force against any passing vehicle that did not maintain a constant speed—never mind actually stopped—outside the fence, Airman Yauk had never heard of any SP actually having to do that. The signs were there to keep curious cars—usually visitors to the base—moving. Yauk's orders were to hold fire unless fired upon or if someone went so far as to penetrate the utility road. The narrow corridor between the outer and inner roads was the death zone. Any unfriendlies caught there were cold meat.

No one had ever been shot in the death zone. And with Pease Air Force Base scheduled to be phased out of existence next year, Airman Yauk figured no one ever would. It made Yauk sad to think that a year from now he'd be stationed somewhere else. But it made him mad to think that even with a year to go, security was getting so slipshod that they weren't bothering to guard the nukes—the officially nonexistent nukes—round the clock.

"What if some terrorist group finds out we're slacking off?" he blurted out loud.

Before Dinan could answer him, his watch alarm buzzed.

"That's it," Dinan chirped. "Midnight. I'm outta here. Coming?"

"I think I'll walk," Airman Henry Yauk said. "You go ahead."

Dinan descended the steps from the huge white guard tower.

Yauk hesitated. He looked out over the array of bunkers once more. From the back, they reminded him of the old Indian burial mounds back in his home state of Missouri. But from the front, the big black double doors set in concrete made him think of modern mausoleums. Either way, the resemblance was appropriate. He wondered again if this had anything to do with the activity at Bunker Number 445.

Earlier in the day, a civilian truck had been admitted into the fence perimeter and something was un-

loaded into Number 445. Yauk, as well as every other
tower SP, had been ordered to keep his eyes averted,
but the activity had been so unusual he couldn't help
but sneak occasional glances at the unloading.

He couldn't see much. The base commander was
there. So was a woman in a dress Air Force uniform.
She had red hair, and the biggest chest this side of
Dolly Parton. There were others. One guy was in his
T-shirt. Yauk figured him for a civilian workman of
some kind, which was unusual. The little Oriental in
native costume broke the "unusual" meter. He was
bizarre. The whole thing was bizarre. You had to have
a secret clearance to work around nukes.

The unloading procedure took over an hour. When
it was done, everyone got into the truck and drove off.
Yauk followed the truck with his eyes, hoping to get a
better look at the redhead with the big jugs.

No such luck. He was surprised not to see her in the
cab. They must have made her ride in the back, which
Yauk thought was pretty fucking unchivalrous of them.
He didn't see the guy in the T-shirt either. Lucky stiff.
He got to ride in back with the girl. Probably asking
her out on a date, too.

Unless, of course, they had been left in the bunker,
which was a ridiculous thought. As ridiculous as leaving the place unguarded overnight.

Reluctantly Airman Yauk descended the tower stairs.
He felt guilty doing so. Some inner voice warned him
that this was bad policy. He had joined the Air Force
in part because of its reputation of being the least
military of the services. There was none of the gung-ho
bullshit you got in the Marines. And it was a damn
sight more prestigious than being in the Army, which
was for grunts anyway. Still, this was plain ridiculous,
he thought as he left the outer fence behind him.

He walked forlornly down the utility road, thankful
for the evening warmth. It was a good ten-minute
walk back to Hemlock Drive, where he lived in one of

the many identical base clapboard quadruplexes. He looked over his shoulder a few times. All was quiet and peaceful. But he couldn't shake the nagging feeling that he was making a mistake in leaving his post without relief, orders or no orders.

Airman Henry Yauk stopped looking back when the low bunkers disappeared around the bend. He wore a worried frown all the way home.

He would have worried more had he lingered five minutes longer.

A ghostly white shape emerged from the Sportsman's Club. Its white skin alive with pulsing golden veinwork, it detached itself like the luminous soul of a haunted house and paused briefly.

It drifted down the road slowly, methodically, through the first electrified fence, without causing sparks to spit or a short circuit, and then passed through the zone of death to the inner fence and beyond.

It stalked toward the array of bunkers, going up to the nearest one. It lingered there a moment, as if looking at the painted number over the massive black doors. Then it passed on to the next grass-sided bunker. It paused at three of the nuclear-weapons storage buildings until it came to the one marked 445.

The shining white being merged with the door, and after it had gone, there was only the soft sighing of a breeze through the well-tended grass.

19

Rair Brashnikov was unaccountably nervous.

Penetrating Pease Air Force Base was a simple matter. Perhaps too simple. He simply drove his rented Cadillac—he always drove Cadillacs because after years of driving a cramped Russian Lada, it was a luxury—past the sweeping entrance to Pease just off the Spaulding Turnpike. The brown sign with its inevitable "Peace Is Our Profession" slogan told him he would soon be approaching exit 4-S. He took 4-S, which whipsawed back on itself, and took a right at a self-service Exxon station. This put him on Nimble Hill Road with its pastoral homes. He followed this until he came to Little Bay Road. He took it and went left on McIntyre Road.

It was nearly midnight. Rair noticed with a frown that while the forest on either side of the road was dense, the trees were very thin and sickly. Many of them had fallen and were leaning against other trees because there was so little open ground. Few standing trees would conceal him in an emergency.

Presently Rair came to a heavily fenced concrete bridge. He pulled over to the side of the road a little way beyond it and got out. The forest looked impenetrable, but not to him. Still, he was astonished at the lax security. The only fence was a series of waist-high metal posts strung with three wide-spaced strands of razor wire.

Perhaps, Brashnikov thought as he doffed his coat to reveal the vibration suit, the Air Force assumed that if no Americans suspected that a public road like this one actually passed through Pease Air Force Base, no foreign agent would. Only a few yards back, the concrete bridge passed over Merrimack Road, which, according to the map provided him, ran past the nuclear-storage bunkers. But Rair would not take that road.

Slipping into the battery-pack harness, he hooked up the cables to his shoulders. He donned the thick gloves. Finally he pulled the helmet over his head and pressed the Velcro flaps closed.

He paused a moment, allowing his eyes to become used to the two-way face membrane. It was like looking through Saran Wrap. The membrane crinkled dryly as his lungs sucked in the confined air and expelled it again.

Then he activated the suit.

He felt the plastic constrict like a straitjacket. He never understood that property, but he had gotten used to it. A faint shine came in through the facial membrane. There was no sound. Electricity flowed through the suit's circuitry and external tubes silently. The crinkling sound ceased too, which was a relief.

The only discomfort was a momentary bone-jarring as the suit achieved its new atomic vibration. Brashnikov's vision swam, and he had to grit his teeth to keep them from chattering. It was a side effect of the suit that required him to have the metal fillings in his teeth replaced twice a year. They kept falling out.

Carefully, because he had to relearn how to walk on his micron-thick boot soles, Brashnikov took a tentative step toward the razor wire. And then into it. His legs went through like milk through a strainer.

Brashnikov plunged into the woods. The first brilliant red and gold leaves of autumn were already on the ground. Although he had no weight, the slight pressure of his soles crushed the dry leaves audibly.

That was not a problem. No one would hear him. It was the pine cones he feared. If he slipped on one, he would doom himself to an eternity of falling through space. Every assignment brought new challenges, taught him new tricks of using the vibration suit.

He passed from the sturdier oaks and spruces carefully, not venturing from each concealing trunk until he stuck his head out to be certain that there were no security police picketed about. It was easy, walking into a tree. Staying inside the trunk was the trick. For it was not simply dark inside. The suit's constant shine dispelled the subatomic darkness. It illuminated the wood that seemed to touch his very corneas. They didn't touch them, of course—nothing could touch them—but the very matter of the wood coexisted with his eyeballs. It made it impossible to keep his eyes open. The blinking reflex screamed protest.

And so Rair Brashnikov would close his eyes before he stepped inside. He paused to steel his nerves and pushed his head forward. When he thought his face had cleared the tree, he opened his black eyes.

Once, in a lightning-blasted pine, he miscalculated and opened his eyes on a rotted cavity swarming with termites. They literally crawled in his face. He shouted his fright, but of course no sound could carry beyond the suit's vibratory aura. He moved on, seeking other shelter.

Brashnikov made his way through the woods in this fashion, staying parallel to Merrimack Road. He came to an open area. Beyond it was the old white house he had been told about, the Sportsman's Club. But the intervening space he would have to clear was open. There was a pond—Peverly Pond, according to his map—and he decided that it would serve him best.

Brashnikov walked stiffly to the edge of the pond and kept going. It was not quite deep enough to conceal him at first. He had to stoop so that the water covered his head. This was the truly frightening part of this penetration. Walking bent over presented him the ever-dreaded risk of losing his balance. If he fell, he would keep on falling. . . .

He walked through the pond, which was not much different from walking through water in a diving suit—except for the distressing tendency of some fishes to swim *into* his helmet.

When he emerged on the other side of the pond, he had a direct walk to the Sportsman's Club. He made for it, crossing the Merrimack Road, which ringed it like a driveway.

The house absorbed him as a sponge absorbs water.

Inside, once certain the place was deserted, Brashnikov turned off the suit. Dusty sheets covered massive furniture. Trophies adorned a cold fieldstone fireplace, and there were plaques on the walls. There were also windows which Brashnikov could use to reconnoiter the weapons-storage bunkers.

From the second floor he saw only the slanting grass-covered backs and sides of the nearest bunkers. They told him nothing. Major Batenin's instructions had suggested the best approach route and the bunker number—445—but nothing more. Still, that was more than Brashnikov had usually received. Often he got only simple marching orders: Go there and steal that. Do not allow yourself to be seen, and above all, avoid capture. It was not easy when the vibration suit sucked so much power from the battery. A nickel-cadmium belt battery would have been better, but Brashnikov would have had to carry several spares with him at all times. It was impractical. But in a country like America, cars—and therefore car batteries—were plentiful. It was just as easy to steal one in an emergency. After two years of experimenting, Brashnikov had come to depend on the Sears DieHard battery.

Brashnikov pulled off one of the thick gauntletlike gloves and checked his watch. Batenin had told him to wait until midnight, when the guard changed. It was nearly nine now. But as his eyes tracked the tall lattice-legged gun tower, and the great open spaces around the security fence, Brashnikov wondered if it would be possible even for him to slip up to Bunker Number 445 unseen. At night the suit's steady glow was like carrying a jack-o'-lantern. Worse, it was like being the jack-o'-lantern.

Brashnikov waited patiently. The guards climbed down off the tower like well-rehearsed spiders, their rifles slung over their shoulders. One came down a little after the other and seemed reluctant to go. But finally he disappeared down the utility road and was gone.

Brashnikov hesitated. Where was their relief? The solitary tower looked deserted, but it was impossible to tell. Its windows were smoked glass.

He decided that the relief team was for some reason delayed. It would be now or never.

Turning on the suit, he emerged from the lodge—first his head, then the rest of him.

Moving in a flat-footed run, he melted through the fence and across the green. The first bunker was Number 443. He moved to the next. It said 444. Good. He kept going until he came to the imposing black double door of Bunker Number 445. It looked like the entrance to some medieval castle with its massive external hinges and locking mechanism.

Brashnikov shut his eyes and put his head in. When he opened them, he saw only subatomic blackness. The gritty interior of the door was in his face. It was obviously a very thick door. He took a chance and walked into it. Craning forward, he opened his eyes again.

The faint shine of the suit illuminated a dark empty space. He stepped in.

He found himself on a bare floor. The walls were a pale gray, like newly poured concrete. A telephone was mounted on a bracket; otherwise the area was empty.

There was another door beyond. It was like an air lock. He walked up and put his head into it.

Rair Brashnikov saw the object of his mission at once.

It stood on a pedestal in the center of the next room. Clearly this room was where nuclear bombs were stored. But there were no nuclear bombs stored here now. Instead two thin spotlights mounted on the ceiling crisscrossed downward to illuminate what looked to be a scale model of a futuristic boomerang-shaped jet. The model was transparent, as if cast in clear Lucite. It had a wingspan of perhaps a dozen feet. Only the wheels, the innards of the transparent dual wing turbines, and the tiny figure of a doll pilot were visible.

According to the briefing Major Batenin had given him, this was a small-scale version of a plane actually in development. It operated by radio control and could in fact turn virtually invisible when powered up and sent aloft, just as later full-scale versions would.

Stealing it should be a simple task, Brashnikov realized. But before he stepped into the vaultlike area, he checked the walls for guards or video cameras.

He saw none. The room was dim, even with the spotlights, which cast only a wan light. There was a hazy quality to the air, as if many people had been smoking in a poorly ventilated room. Brashnikov noticed one peculiar thing. Tall bluish mirrors hung on three of the walls, one to each wall. They reflected the bizarre sight of his glowing soap bubble of a face sticking to the wall like a leech.

Satisfied that the mirrors were harmless, Rair Brashnikov stepped all the way into the room. He walked carefully to the pedestal. The details of the craft, as he got nearer, were exquisite.

"*Krahseevah*," he breathed in admiration, suddenly wishing that there were two planes. He would enjoy having such a toy for himself. But keeping this one for himself was out of the question. Batenin would kill him. Literally.

Brashnikov stopped before the pedestal. He looked around one more time, uneasily. He felt eyes upon him. But again, he was certain there were no video cameras. And he was obviously alone. Except for the pedestal-mounted model and the tall wall mirrors, the room was bare.

He turned off the suit. The fabric loosened and the unpleasant vibration in his teeth came and went quickly.

Smiling beneath his crinkling membrane of a helmet, he reached for the aircraft model.

His heart leapt up into his throat. His fingers went right through it!

Brashnikov tried again. But again, his hands merged with the craft's hull unfeelingly.

Frowning, he wondered if the suit was still somehow operating. Perhaps he hadn't turned it off all the way. He forced the rheostat angrily.

Now it was off for certain. He grabbed for the plane. But again his hands touched only air.

His unease rising, Rair Brashnikov turned the rheostat the other way. He felt the familiar vibration anew. Okay, he thought to himself, suit is operating. I must remain calm. This should be simple. Now I will simply turn suit off.

He twisted the rheostat the other way. The vibration ceased. Brashnikov reached for the aircraft. His fingers touched it. But they felt nothing. He clenched his hands, but the model stayed in place. Nothing he did disturbed it. Its gleaming immobility seemed to mock him.

Rair Brashnikov felt a ringing in his ears. Something was wrong. Something was terribly wrong. He was insubstantial no matter what he did. What had gone wrong? Was the suit malfunctioning? Was it about to go nuclear? Or—and this somehow seemed to him infinitely more terrible than going up in a boiling ball of atomic fire—had his body become stuck in the vibratory pattern of the suit? Was he doomed to forever walk the earth a living ghost? It was too horrible to contemplate.

Brashnikov had no time to contemplate the possibility any longer, for on opposite walls two of the blue floor-length mirrors shattered with a single sound.

Brashnikov wheeled. He saw the tiny Oriental in black coming at him, his skirts flying, his face tight with anger.

Recoiling from the violence of the impending attack, Brashnikov reached for the belt rheostat. Out of the corner of one eye he caught his reflection in the remaining mirror. It was still intact, although it was shaking violently. His mind absorbed the split-second image of a man with dead eyes coming up behind him, two linked fingers driving for his shoulder like a striking cobra.

His heart high in his mouth, Brashnikov turned the control.

Too late! He felt the pain of impact. He screamed. His vision went red as he clutched at his pain-seared shoulder. The agony was unendurable. It felt as if the ball-and-socket joint had exploded, sending bone splinters flying into every muscle and nerve he possessed.

His vision cleared instantly, just in time for him to see the man with the dead eyes carried through his own chest with the momentum of his attack. That, and that alone, told Rair Brashnikov that despite the incredible pain, the man had just grazed him.

And the suit was operating!

The Oriental was upon him next. Fingernails tore at his face, his chest, his hands. They passed through him harmlessly, but something in their very fury filled Brashnikov with fear.

All thoughts of his mission gone from his mind, Brashnikov frantically flailed around. He must escape. He moved toward the third mirror, but it came apart

to reveal a recess in the wall and a redheaded woman
in an Air Force blue dress uniform.

She was firing at him. The bullets passed through
him, but Brashnikov dared not take any chances with
the suit malfunctioning so strangely.

He stepped quickly toward the other room. He remembered the wall telephone there. That would be his
escape. He dared not engage the two men—he recognized them as his adversaries from two earlier encounters
—in a game of hide-and-seek. He knew now that their
powers and stamina would outlast his battery—DieHard
or not.

Brashnikov emerged on the other side of the wall.
The telephone gleamed like a faint beacon. It looked
like any telephone, but to Rair Brashnikov it was a
lifeline to safety.

The air-lock door reverberated with a pounding like
sledgehammers, echoes bouncing off the bare walls.
But in Brashnikov's panicky imagination, he did not
see the pair taking sledgehammers to the opposite
side. He saw them beating on it with bare fists. Bumps
appeared on Brashnikov's side. They were fist-size
bumps.

Brashnikov turned off the suit and with a prayer on
his quivering lips reached out for the phone.

"*Raduysa Mariye, blagodati poliaya, Gospod s't'voyu
. . .*" he whispered, surprised that the old words came
so easily from memory.

He felt the pressure of the gray plastic receiver
against the thick material of his gloves, and tears of
relief jumped from his eyes. He was solid! He could
use the phone!

Brashnikov dialed the Soviet embassy in Washington with frantic stabs of his gloved fingers as the
air-lock door behind him started to protest as it was
forced out of its frame by an increasing machine-gun
volley of blows. He hesitated. Had he just hit five? Or
four? It should have been five. Should he hang up and

start over? The air-lock door screeched horribly. He kept dialing. There was no time to waste. Even if he had misdialed, anyplace would be better than here.

He heard the first ring.

Then the door flew out. It came at him like a truck.

Brashnikov turned the rheostat hard.

He saw the skinny white man and the Oriental leap into the room, and then everything went white. Brashnikov wanted to shout at them. Too late, too late, Americans! But it was too late even for gloating.

Everything was all right. Everything would be all right.

Rair Brashnikov found himself hurtling through a dark tunnel. Voices sounded in his head. He listened, trying to separate a Russian accent from the babble of English. But all he heard was the insistent ringing of a telephone somewhere—far, far away.

He prayed that the switchboard operator would answer soon. She seemed to be taking an obscenely long time.

20

"We're getting nowhere," Remo Williams snapped hotly, stepping away from the door. "We're supposed to be a team. Let's see some teamwork."

"We are already too late," the Master of Sinanju fumed.

"Then we're trying to beat one another to something that isn't there anymore. So come on."

Remo and Chiun set themselves before the battered air-lock door. Together they slammed their palms into the center of the door. It jumped from its frame as if shot from a cannon.

They leapt into the room.

"There!" Remo said, seeing the *Krahseevah* frantically punching numbers on the keypad. He flew at him, hoping this time he wouldn't be too late. He knew he had touched the Russian's shoulder in the split second before the suit had activated. It was like touching a frustratingly elusive mirage—which of course the *Krahseevah* had been in every previous encounter. And although Remo had inflicted damage, he had not incapacitated the Russian. He wanted another crack at him.

But the Master of Sinanju had other ideas. "It is my turn," he cried.

"He's up for grabs," Remo growled.

They converged on the *Krahseevah* just as his glow-

ing form misted over and was hungrily gobbled up by
the telephone receiver. Their reaching hands grasped
and clutched at the nebulous white shape as it collapsed and was drawn away. But to no avail. The last
tendrils that were the *Krahseevah*'s hand entered the
mouthpiece, and it was gone.

Chiun caught the receiver as it fell.

"We are too late," he said angrily.

"Give me that," Remo said, taking the receiver
away from him and clapping it to one ear. He listened
anxiously as Robin Green, reloading a smoking automatic, stepped into the room.

"You lied to me," she said harshly. "You tricked
me!"

"Quiet," Remo said, listening. He heard crackling
static, and under it, the steady ringing of a telephone
on the other end.

"Great," he said, punching a button on the telephone. He got another line and pressed the pound
button continuously. A relay triggered an automatic
dialing sequence, and soon Remo was hearing another
phone ringing.

The receiver was picked up on the other end.

"Yes?" a dry voice said.

"Smitty. He got away from us. But he's coming
your way."

"I know. The special phone is ringing," Dr. Harold
W. Smith said.

In the background, Remo heard a telephone jangling.

"Yeah, I can hear it too," Remo said. "What do
you want us to do?"

"I will handle this," Smith told him. "Tie up any
loose ends and return to Folcroft." The line went
dead.

In his office at Folcroft Sanitarium Dr. Harold W.
Smith replaced the receiver. He turned his attention to
another telephone, one which sat beside it. It was a

standard AT&T desk model, unusual only in that it
had no dial or push buttons. But this wasn't the dialless
telephone that was Smith's direct link to the White
House. That phone was red. This one was gray. The
gray telephone kept ringing. Smith ignored it and turned
in his cracked leather swivel chair.

He stooped at the baseboard where the ringing telephone connected to a wall jack. Smith took the round
plug in his hands and pulled the prongs from the jack.

Abruptly, the gray telephone stopped ringing.

Smith returned to his desk, his thin lips quirked into
a rare dry-as-dust smile.

"You turkeys tricked me!" Robin Green repeated.

"Hey, you had your chance," Remo told her defensively.

"I almost didn't get out from behind my mirror. It
was supposed to shatter at a single blow."

"Gee, mine shattered the first time," Remo said in
a dubious tone. "How about yours, Little Father?"

"My mirror broke easily," Chiun said smugly.

"I meant a normal blow!" Robin shouted, face
flushed. "I kept pounding and pounding. Finally, I
had to shoot my way out."

"Everyone knows that women are weak," Chiun
sniffed. "I am sure that had you been born a male,
you would have had no trouble breaking your mirror."

Robin Green looked at them with smoldering blue
eyes. Her knuckles whitened on the butt of her automatic. Remo thought for a moment that she was going
to open up on them. Instead, she sucked in a deep
breath, as if to get control of herself. A button on her
dress-blue uniform popped and hit the floor noisily.

She looked down at it. "Oh, I give up," she said in
a small defeated voice. She slumped up against the
wall. "Just tell me what happened here, okay?"

"You saw it through your two-way mirror," Remo
said, returning the button, "just as we did. The

Krahseevah panicked. He thought the suit wasn't working, so we went for him while he was switching back and forth."

"And you were too slow," Chiun said shortly.

"Hey, I touched him. I hurt him," Remo retorted. "Which is more than I can say for some people around here."

"If you are referring to me, my place of concealment was further away from that creature than yours. You had an unfair advantage. No doubt you were abetted by the whites who constructed this snare under Emperor Smith's direction."

"Same distance. We measured them, remember? You insisted."

Robin stamped her foot suddenly.

"Will you two stop it!" she scolded. "We lost him. Probably for good, this time. All I want is something plausible to put into my report. Maybe I can still salvage what's left of my career."

"Uh-uh, not for good," Remo said. "I'll admit I would have preferred to capture him with my bare hands, but Smith knew that that was an iffy proposition at best. So he had a backup plan in place."

"Whoa, go back two squares. What about this?" Robin asked, pointing to the model.

They crowded around the model aircraft.

"Go ahead, touch it," Remo suggested.

Her brows puckering, Robin Green reached out with both hands. They passed through the model as if it were a mirage.

She looked at Remo in slack-jawed amazement. Remo indicated the ceiling lights with a finger.

"It's a hologram," he explained. "A three-dimensional image projected by lasers. It's not real. Never was."

"You could have told me that before you sealed me behind that chickshit mirror."

Remo shrugged. "No time. Besides, you're still recovering from the car crash. We couldn't risk you getting hurt."

"Hey. I'm as good as any man. I've proved that."

The Master of Sinanju walked over to a corner where a little brass censer squatted. Stooping, he sprinkled white powder onto dimly smoldering coals. With a noxious puff of smoke, the coals went out.

Chiun brought the censer back to the pedestal and presented it to Robin Green with a twinkle in his hazel eyes. She accepted it wordlessly.

"What's this?" she asked at last. "I don't understand."

"There was a little bit of a problem with the laser image," Remo explained. "We tested it before we brought it here and it flickered like film going through a bad projector. We didn't know what to do until Chiun came up with a solution."

Chiun's papery lips broke into a satisfied smile.

"Blue mirrors and smoke," he explained, gesturing through the haze to the shattered blue-tinted mirrors whose dangling shards framed closetlike wall recesses. "You had it backward, which is typical for someone who has had the misfortune to be born both white and female."

"He's teasing you," Remo told Robin.

"About what? Being female or the other nonsense? And why are you grinning?" Robin demanded, looking for a place to put the censer down. She tried to set it to one side of the aircraft model, but there was no room. Finally she muttered, "Oh, the hell with it," and set it squarely atop the hologram aircraft. The combined object looked like a brass bowl with glass wings.

"Because it's all over," Remo said pleasantly.

"What do you mean, all over? He got away. Again."

"Nope," Remo said, escorting her to the wall telephone.

"Did you ever hear of a telephone being installed in a nuclear-weapons storage bunker?" Remo asked.

"No. I may be a service brat, but I didn't exactly grow up in one of these things."

" 'Brat' is the word," Chiun sniffed.

"Another piece of Smith's handiwork," Remo said, picking up the receiver. "No matter which number you dial"—he demonstrated by hitting several keys at random—"it's programmed to ring only one phone in the entire world. A special one on Smith's desk."

"Oh, he has a desk, does he?" Robin said sarcastically. "And here I thought he lived in a padded room with all the other lunatics who think they're Napoleon. Don't think I missed Charlie Chan here calling him emperor. Or you calling *him* Little Father. I must have been crazy to try to work with you two. No, I take that back. I must be the only sane one around here. Just give me that."

Robin took the receiver. Brushing away a bit of hair, she put it to her ear.

"I don't hear anything," she said.

"That's good," Remo said. "It means Smith disconnected the phone at the other end."

Robin blinked as the significance of Remo's words penetrated.

"Disconnected?"

"Yep," Remo said with a self-satisfied grin.

"So where's the *Krahseevah*?" Robin asked uncertainly.

"Got me," Remo said casually, hanging up the phone. "But he didn't come out on Smith's end. He didn't come back. My guess is that he's somewhere in the coils of Ma Bell. You know, I once saw a commercial that claimed there are billions and billions of miles of cable in our telephone system. I think our *Krahseevah*'s in for a long, long roller-coaster ride."

"And just to make certain . . ." Chiun said, stepping up to the phone. He took the device in one hand and began squeezing. The edges of the phone wavered and

collapsed. Tiny jets of smoke spurted from the ruptur-
ing seams.

When the Master of Sinanju extracted the phone
from the wall, it was a blob of plastic. He slapped it
into Robin Green's hands. She said "Ouch!" and tossed
it from hand to hand like a hot potato.

"What's the idea?"

"A souvenir," Chiun told her. "For your grandchildren."

"I don't have any grandchildren. Hell, I don't even
have children."

"Ah, but you will," Chiun said, indicating her cleavage, which strained at her remaining buttons. "For
you carry your destiny proudly before you."

Robin turned to Remo. "Is that Korean for 'bare-
foot and pregnant'?" she asked.

"He's teasing you again," Remo assured her.

"How about it, buster?" Robin asked Chiun. "Are
you pulling my leg?"

"No. I leave the pulling of your legs to the future
father of your children." Chiun bowed. "May you
bear many squalling infants," he intoned.

"Well, that's it," Remo said quickly, edging for the
door.

"That's it?" Robin said shakily.

"What else is there? We bagged him."

"It is not as good as a bird in the hand," Chiun told
Robin solemnly. "But neither is it two in the bush."

"What's that supposed to mean?"

Chiun shrugged. "I thought you would know. You
who are so fond of sayings concerning birds."

"Is he kidding me? He *is* kidding, isn't he?"

"Don't worry about it," Remo told her. "We gotta
go now. Been nice working with you."

Robin blocked his way. "Go! You just hold your
horses. What about me? I got you onto this base. You
can't leave me hanging out to dry. For a third time."

Remo picked Robin up bodily and set her aside like a coat rack.

"You won't be," he said. "And you didn't help get us onto the base. We only let you think that. Once you baited the trap, you were just window dressing."

"But what about me? What about my career?" Robin demanded, following them out of the bunker.

"Everything's been taken care of. Don't sweat it."

"Taken care of—by whom?"

"Smith, of course. He's fixed your files. You're not AWOL, and all is forgiven. In fact, there's a pretty good chance that you're going to be offered an Air Force commission. But there's a catch. You can't mention me or Chiun or Smith in your report. Otherwise not only will there be no commission, but your goose—if you'll pardon the expression—will be cooked."

"What! That's impossible. You're lying to me again. Smith couldn't possibly do all that. He's a civilian. Even my father couldn't pull that many strings."

"Hey, don't thank us. We're just doing our job."

"If you're lying to me," Robin shouted after them, "I won't let you get away with this. Do you hear me?"

"Do I hear her?" Remo muttered as they hurried away. "Smith can probably hear her clear down to Folcroft."

"True," Chiun said. "She has an amazing set of lungs—for a woman."

"Oh, really." Remo smiled. "And how, exactly, do you mean that, Little Father?"

"In the spirit it is intended, of course."

"Of course."

A week later, Remo was in his kitchen boiling rice. A familiar knock sounded at the back door, and before Remo could say, "Come in," Harold W. Smith did.

"You're getting to be a pretty casual neighbor,"

Remo told him. "Maybe we should get you your own key."

"Er, sorry, Remo," Smith mumbled, adjusting his glasses. "I have only a moment."

"Then you won't mind if I don't ask you to sit down and join us?" Remo returned as he poured the rice into a woven rattan colander. He shook it to drain away the last steaming water.

"Of course not," Smith said, standing in the doorway as if unwilling to trespass further.

Remo tapped a small brass gong over the stove. It reverberated solemnly. "Good," he said. "I only cooked for two."

Chiun swept into the door, saw the rice, and then saw Smith. His placid expression flickered into momentary annoyance. Then, like the sun breaking through clouds, a smile beamed from his pleasantly wrinkled face.

"Ah, Emperor," he said. "You are just in time to join us in a simple repast."

"There's only enough for us," Remo put in quickly.

"Nonsense," Chiun replied. "Remo will have his meal later."

"Chiun . . ." Remo warned.

"It is all right, Remo," Chiun said, pulling out a chair for Smith. "Come, Emperor. I insist."

"Actually, I've eaten," Smith told him, accepting the seat. "I merely wanted to brief you on the aftermath of the *Krahseevah* matter."

"Then you may do so and observe how the Sinanju assassin ekes out his pitiful existence. Remo, serve, please."

As Remo ladled out helpings of unseasoned brown rice onto two china plates, Chiun launched into a running commentary.

"Notice the simple fare," he told Smith. "Rice. Only rice."

"I understand that rice is the staple of the Sinanju diet," Smith said uncomfortably.

"Ah, but we are also allowed to eat duck, and certain fish. Do you see any fish on this meager table?"

"No," Smith admitted.

"I am certain that the Boston Red Sox are eating fish even as we speak. Even the lowliest of them. The ones who are so poorly paid that they earn as much as other menials. Like atomic scientists, brain surgeons, and that underappreciated but necessary minority, the assassin."

"Master of Sinanju, I must tell you in all frankness that you are exceedingly well-paid for your work."

"True," Chiun said simply as Remo sat down and dug into his rice. "I am better paid than the Master who came before me. But he lived in evil times. I am privileged to live in an era when riches are bestowed on persons in all manner of ridiculous professions. I read only the other day that that talk-show woman, Copra Inisfree, is paid millions for her services. Have you ever watched her program, Emperor?"

"No, not really."

Chiun leaned closer. "Most of the time she just sits," he said in a hushed voice. "I would like an assignment where I might simply sit and speak with boon companions, basking in the applause of others."

"I don't think you quite grasp the complex economics here, Master Chiun. As with baseball games, *The Copra Inisfree Show* is sponsored by commercial firms. They pay her fabulous sums because of the audience she attracts, which in turn purchase their products."

"Then I will attract an audience!" Chiun cried. "It will be the biggest audience the world has ever seen! We will sell their products and we will all become rich men."

Smith looked to Remo helplessly.

Remo took a sip of mineral water in an effort to keep a straight face.

"Our work is secret," Smith said stiffly. "You know that."

"But our sponsor is the greatest sponsor in the land. The President of the United States. Surely his coffers can spare a few more gold ingots."

"Please, Master of Sinanju. I have only a few minutes. We can discuss this later. After all, your current contract has nearly another year to run."

"Perhaps you are right. Excuse me while I allow myself a sip of purified water, for it is the only beverage I can afford on my present salary."

Smith sighed. When Chiun put down the glass, he resumed speaking.

"I have been reviewing CIA intercepts of message traffic out of the Soviet embassy down in Washington," he said. "The post is in an uproar. They have not heard from their agent at all."

"That means we've seen the last of the *Krahseevah*, right?" Remo said through a mouthful of rice.

"So it would seem. They've given up on him and recalled their chargé d'affaires to Moscow. Evidently, as his case officer, he will bear the brunt of the responsibility and the punishment for what happened."

"So what did happen to the *Krahseevah*? Is he dead?"

"I don't really know," Smith admitted. "Going on the assumption that his nuclear constituents were being carried by electrical impulse through the phone system to my telephone, the act of unplugging it before the connection was made could have caused any number of consequences. Perhaps his atoms are still racing through the system. Perhaps they've been scattered or destroyed. When dealing with experimental technology such as this, it's impossible to say. The bottom line is that he's no longer a threat and the Soviets have lost their unrestricted access to U.S. technology. Just in time, too. They may have plundered key parts of our Stealth technology, but without sample RAM tiles to replicate, they might as well be trying to build an operational plane from a child's plastic model kit."

"You know, I just realized something," Remo said. "Except for the *Krahseevah*—and you actually took care of him—we didn't have to kill anyone this time out."

Hearing this, Chiun dropped a forkful of rice.

"Do not hold this against us, Emperor," he said loudly. "I promise you that this will never happen again. You will have bodies in plenty during our next assignment. For an assassin's worth is truly measured by the blood he spills, and I promise you that soon your swimming pool will brim with the blood of America's enemies."

"But I don't own a swimming pool," Smith protested.

"Have one built. Remo and I will supply the blood."

"Please," Smith said. "I'm just as happy that this assignment produced no unnecessary casualties. Now, if you'll excuse me, I must be going."

"Let me see you to the door," Chiun said, getting up.

Smith looked at the dozen or so feet that separated him from the back door. The distance suddenly looked to be a mile long. "As you wish," he said unhappily.

Guiding Smith by the elbow, Chiun escorted him to the door.

"I have been watching these baseball games with Remo. It is always the same. Boston beats Detroit and then Detroit savagely attacks Chicago. This is exactly the kind of intercity warfare that brought down the Greek Empire. Let me suggest that Remo and I pay secret visits to the rulers of these recalcitrant city-states. We will force them to mend their ways. Perhaps in this way the union may endure another two hundred brief years and the President will be so grateful that he will offer to raise your salary, and you in turn might see fit to increase the tribute paid to my house." Chiun paused to stroke his facial hair thought-

fully. He measured Smith's aghast expression out of
the corner of his eye and went on.

"Of course, it is only a suggestion," he said dismissively.
"But I know you will see the wisdom of not allowing
America to tear itself apart in such an unseemly and
public fashion."

Smith nodded mutely. Just two more steps . . . he
thought numbly. It was like walking the last mile.

"You perhaps do not realize that this baseball warfare has spread beyond your shores," Chiun went on.
"The Japanese have fallen into settling their differ-
ences in this manner as well. It is a plague. But if we
work together on this, we will both profit."

Remo's uncontrollable laughter followed them out
into the backyard.

Epilogue

Crackle.

". . . So, Cinzia. Wanna *whoosh* tonight?"

"I don't *crackle* know. Will you respect me in the morning?"

"I don't respect you now." *Crackle.* Tomorrow can only be an improvement." *Whoosh.*

"Oh, you! You always make me laugh." *Whoosh.* "Sure. Dinner first?"

"How about Legal *sput* Seafoods? Haven't eaten there in a *crackle.*"

"*Help!*"

"Hey, do you hear that?"

"What?"

"Something on the line."

"This is a *crackle* staticky *pop* line."

"No. It wasn't static. It was a strange voice. Like *'whoosh.'* "

"Say again? I didn't catch that last part."

"I said, it's like we're on a party line."

"Maybe your phone's being tapped."

"No. Shhh. Listen."

"Help, help! I am trapped in telephone line. Some-one help me."

"Hear it now?"

"Yeah. Funny accent *pop crackle* don't you think? Sounds Russian."

"Hey, maybe it's the KGB."

"Why would they tap my line?"

"It's probably *crackle* a crossed wire."

"Help me. Help me. Help me."

"He sounds *real* unhappy."

"Get real, Cinz. It's only someone playing with their *sput*."

"I don't know. That's real panic in his voice."

"Oh, come on. 'Help me, I'm trapped in telephone line'? Reminds *whoosh* of that stupid fortune you got when I took you to the Cathay Pacific last *crackle*. You know, the one that said, 'Help, I'm being held prisoner in a fortune *pop* cookie factory.' "

"You're right. What could I be thinking of?"

"So . . . pick you up, say, sevenish?"

"Hmmm. Better make it eight. I'm going to run out and buy a new phone. This one's been acting *sput* a lot. As you can hear."

"Yeah. Things sure haven't been *crackle* since Ma Bell broke up."

Whoosh. "Tell me about it. *Ciao.*"

The tunnel walls zoomed by. They seemed to go on forever. And all Rair Brashnikov could imagine was that this time he truly was dead. This time the dark tunnel was not a fiberoptic cable. And soon he would see the silvery light that would bring him peace.

But as he rushed along endlessly, Brashnikov felt only a wild, numbing panic. If this were truly the path to heaven, why were all the voices American?